# S.

# Typewriter

*by*

# Harrison Matthews

PublishAmerica
Baltimore

At the specific preference of the author, PublishAmerica allowed this work to remain exactly as the author intended, verbatim, without editorial input.

This book is a work of fiction. Names, characters, places, and incidents are products of the author's imagination or are used fictitiously. Any resemblance to actual events or locales or persons, living or dead, is entirely coincidental.

ISBN: 1-4241-5500-2
PUBLISHED BY PUBLISHAMERICA, LLLP
www.publishamerica.com
Baltimore

Printed in the United States of America

I dedicate this book to a good friend, to a friend who has been supportive and encouraging since the beginning. His name is Greg Lindholm.

I would like to acknowledge the following for their assistance in preparing this book: Mark Nygaard, for his optimism and the use of his scanner; John Beeson, for helping prepare the text and also not strangling me; Jon Springer, for taking the photograph on the back cover; and Lenore Barry for her generosity.

# BOOK ONE

# THE MYTH OF THE OPENING SENTENCE

# 1.

It was a form letter, my name appearing in dark type behind "Dear." The author of the letter, Robert Sheckley, fiction editor of *Omni* magazine, regretfully informed me that the enclosed material did not suit their needs at this time. He was therefore returning it. I was asked to excuse such an impersonal reply, the volume of submissions Mr. Sheckley received making this procedure a sad necessity. My interest in *Omni* was greatly appreciated, and, indeed, I was to keep them in mind for future manuscripts. Mr. Sheckley closed with "regrets."

The letter was dated December 28th, 1979. It was now the third of January. Having been out of town the past two weeks, I had no way of knowing if the manuscript had arrived during the old year or the new. This was important. Submitting stories to magazines had caused a section of my psyche to historically regress, to abandon the rationality of the modern era and adopt all the superstitions of medieval occultism. Was the rejected manuscript a sign of things past or yet to come?

I stood for several minutes in the foyer of my apartment building, sorting through the bills and Christmas cards, the circulars from Sears and K-Mart and Hardware Hank, that comprised the remainder of my mail, gleaning what consolation I could in having at least received an answer. For, though, the answer had come via the mute blow of a rejection letter, the "sad necessity" Mr. Sheckley acknowledged, it was in its way cathartic, would ultimately instill nothing less than renewed determination.

Or so I hoped. I had spent New Year's Eve on a Greyhound bus, returning from rural Arkansas to urban Minneapolis, hurtling insanely north into the grey teeth of winter. At midnight the driver flicked the interior lights, wishing a happy new year over the intercom. I deemed it an Orwellian welcome to an Orwellian era. Gone were the dreams of a generation, or if not gone then assimilated, and I had never felt more alone with my resources, my resolve.

Six months earlier my cousin asked me to leave his home. I had come to his door upon completing yet another of my "on the road" excursions, living under his family's largess while I looked for work. Though my cousin was three years younger than me, he was in every other way much older, possessing all the accouterments of adulthood I disdained: a split-level suburban rambler, a large green lawn, a year-old Buick. That I was at best an interloper, more likely a transgressor, in this tidy universe had to be pointed out by my cousin himself. Perhaps I would be more comfortable, he said one Sunday morning as I flattened out Blondie and Dagwood on the kitchen table, my cousin clearing his throat, his wife glancing at him expectantly, perhaps I would be more comfortable if I moved into a place of my own. I could not blame him. Indeed, after the initial embarrassment, I was in many ways grateful. This was the kick in the ass I needed. I, too, could enter the land of maturity and responsibility, of success, but I would do so on my own terms.

I rented a sleeping room in Northeast Minneapolis that day, later in the week procuring a part-time job as a night janitor. In less than a month I found myself telling a stranger I was a writer.

This happened at Momart's Tavern, a corner bar three blocks from my room. I stopped there one afternoon by way of celebration — my first story intended for publication lay at the bottom of a mailbox on Nineteenth and Central, as good as on its way to the offices of *Playboy*. Pushing through the double aluminum doors, I saw there were but three old men huddled at the end of the bar, intent on a game of cribbage. They fit right in. Momart's itself was old, with a high arabesque ceiling, oval mirrors and an abundance of polished wood. As with many of the businesses along Central Avenue, Momart's gleaned no small part of its income from denizens of the senior citizen monolith a few blocks to the east. These venerable citizens were everywhere — restaurants, drugstores, bus stops — and I had taken to covertly studying them, as though to discern my own future. Feeling expansive this warm windy afternoon, I bought a round of beers for the house.

This was less magnanimous than it sounds. Momart's was a three-two bar, selling watery beer for about half the price of the stronger stuff. Still, the gesture seldom went unappreciated. The three old men toasted me in ragged unison, and, as I had somewhat expected, one of them ambled over.

He was tall and thick, with a pasty complexion. "Don Dunn's my name and fun's my game," he said, extending a meaty hand. After hearing my name and pumping my hand, Mr. Dunn stood very close, his ample stomach brushing against mine. He examined me with pale-blue eyes for several seconds, then asked, "What're you in for?"

"Life," I answered, having no idea what he meant.

"Life! Ha! I love it. We're all in for life."

Wheezing like a bicycle pump, Mr. Dunn placed an arm around my shoulders, cupping my ear with his free hand and rolling his eyes towards the bartender in histrionic display. In a stage whisper loud enough to overcome the jukebox, a whisper replete with the odors of beer, tobacco and tooth decay, Mr. Dunn said, "We'll all probably die in this stinking hole."

I essayed that one could do worse, actually using "one" as a pronoun instead of "you." Mr. Dunn stepped back as though appraising me.

"What do you do?" he asked.

"I'm a writer," I answered, for the first time in my life.

Mr. Dunn slapped his palm on the bar, roaring for two more beers. Fearing that Mr. Dunn—thick, pasty, ebullient Mr. Dunn—was about to impart, if not his entire life story, then at least significant chunks of it, I began mentally composing excuses to leave. Though having for the first time flatly stated my calling, I'd found ample occasion to let the information "slip" out, couching the language to imply that, though I had yet to earnestly try for publication, such a fate was no doubt just beyond the horizon. Since these disclosures usually occurred at bars and late-night parties, my ears were often assaulted by epic-length, multi-tangented personal histories, recitations all too quickly devolving into incoherent mutterings, all too reminiscent of my own scrawlings. I promised to drink only one beer with Mr. Dunn, listen to one episode, then leave.

"Joe," said Mr. Dunn, his arm again round my shoulders, the bartender walking up with two more beers, "did you know my friend here is a writer?"

Mr. Dunn's voice, most likely never accused of being subdued, entered one of those strange synchronizations of silence, the jukebox between records, the traffic outside still, the cribbage game finished, causing all to look at, not Mr. Dunn, but me. I smiled moronically back, as if I were some hapless foreigner passing but briefly through their land. No one pursued the issue, asking questions about published works or other such dreary details. And Mr. Dunn, contrary to my fears, did not impart his life story but instead, after obscenely commenting on the temperature of the beer, ambled off to play the winner of the cribbage game. I drank my beer alone and eventually left, unnoticed.

What bothered me later that night, hunched over my Underwood and working on my second story (oh, I was a go-getter), was the nonreaction to Mr. Dunn's announcement. Had the old men jeered, laughed, threatened violence, it would have been less unsettling than their apathy. Had my entry into the realm of struggling writers been such a perfect dive, causing but the faintest of ripples?

The decision to write had not been made hastily. Though warned of the eons of apprenticeship facing would-be authors, I'd had little doubt my case would prove an exception. I was not some idealistic English major, after all, but a man facing the end of his third decade. And I was not simply jumping Gaugin-like into my task. For two years I had filled spiral notebooks with spontaneous and unchecked ramblings, marijuana-induced poetry, travel journals, remembered conversations. Writing had been "fun," and my immediate goal, that of bequeathing stories upon magazines while basking in monetary and laudatory remuneration, seemed not inordinately out of reach.

As with many decisions in my life, this one had been made with a great deal of thought and no logic. Attempting to break into the field via its most difficult form, the short story, did not for a moment dissuade me. The plan was so simple. After a few stories and articles, pieces that would no doubt start portentous rumblings in the literary world, I would then (having gotten the hang of this writing business) create The Novel. After that came the good life, a hazy montage of first-class airline cabins, the polished mahogany of publisher's desks, a succession of well-received books, the skylines of Manhattan, Rome, Rio...

Plus, I had something to prove. My cousin's soft-spoken eviction had seemed, despite his assurance otherwise, an indictment not only of me but of my aspirations. I had talked about writing for a living long enough. Now, with steely determination, I was going to do it. Oh Matthews! Were not for blind meandering, there would be no art!

Using my cousin's van (for we had not severed all ties), I moved what belongings I had into my new residence. I had sold or given away most of my possessions before my last trip, viewing the event, as always, as less a vacation than catharsis. This was just as well. My apartment was little more than one room posing as two. A sink, kitchenette and bulbous refrigerator inhabited one side, the other serving as bedroom, parlor and study. A communal bathroom was down the hall. The building itself was a squat, multi-gabled structure, a profusion of additions obscuring its original shape. Painted the color of Caucasian flesh, the trim an olive green, it rose fully three stories from the earth. I was intimidated upon first seeing the house and almost didn't go in. What Usherian perils lay waiting?

The landlady was a tall thin women named Mrs. McAdams. She lived in the basement midst water pipes and heating ducts, a metal-framed bed alongside the furnace and a gas cooking range alongside that. Mrs. McAdams had taken me down there on my initial visit, conducting her version of an interview before showing me the available rooms. I stood, arms behind my back (rather like *parade rest*), while she sat on the edge of her bed, a cigarette aimed from her mouth, her attitude less inquisitive than inquisitorial.

She was, in her own words, a tough old broad who had thrown out grown men in the middle of the night, and any violation of the house rules promised swift retribution. Did I drink excessively? No. Would I be having loud parties? No. Would girls be staying over? I hesitated. "Sometimes?"

prompted Mrs. McAdams. "Sometimes," I said (if I were lucky).

My room was on the second floor and had but one window. Beyond the window was the brick wall of a hardware store, shunting all but the most indirect light. This was good—less distraction. I found four cement blocks, apparently left by the previous tenant, and placed them on end in the center of what Mrs. McAdams called the living room. Atop this podium went the Underwood. A small bean-bag chair, my sole article of furniture, went before the podium. The hardwood floor would serve as desktop. And for now, this was all I needed.

# 2.

Why did I send my first story to *Playboy*? Other writers have told me of similarly ambitious targets for their first-ever submissions, assaulting the *New Yorker*, the *Atlantic*, *Harper's* with strained metaphors and underworked verbiage, stilted dialogue and clumsy characters (clumsy like colts!). Of course, the availability is appealing. Why bat in the minor leagues when you can swing in Yankee Stadium? To live in the present is to forfeit perspective, and though I knew, intellectually, of the thousand other writers tapping in the American night, I did not know of them, would not hear that tapping till an ancient night in early January, the night of the *Omni* rejection.

Besides prestige (I could not wait to allude to my "latest" story in Playboy) was the matter of money. According to the 1979 *Writer's Market*, *Playboy* paid three thousand dollars for a short story, by far the most attractive offer listed. I could live for months off one sale.

There was another reason for deigning *Playboy* the vehicle of my debut. Though I seldom bought the magazine anymore, I had once done so — I want to say "religiously" — during my "college" years (having attended not one minute of one class, I nonetheless shared a house near the University of Minnesota with several students, experiencing the good side of college life — parties, sex, drugs — while avoiding its more mundane aspects), and many of my contemporaries were similarly smitten with, if not *Playboy*, then *Penthouse* or *Hustler* or some like publication. Certainly much of the attraction was sex, or at least the portrayal of sex, the unobtainable woman now yours, a paper obtainment, the glossy pages displaying a lifestyle composed not only of taut buttocks and inflated breasts but of Alfa Romeo sports cars, Cardin watches, Ralph Lauren shirts, the magazine's flattering assumption that you the reader are a hip young man, certainly on the way up, and the good life, if not yours already, is but over the horizon, around the corner, in tomorrow's mail.

And I believed this. But with the passing of years came a tempering, a realization that if the women of glossy pages existed, they were in a land I would never venture. The women I encountered were notoriously unPlayboy-like. Many of them had cellulite, pimples, bad breath, some nagged, or farted in bed, were true, untrue, stupid, smart, sexy, maddening, and all evoked emotions beyond the simplicity of passion. The other promise, that of the bejeweled chronograph and glistening convertible, also remained unfulfilled (was I really the type of man who read *Playboy*?), and in time the myth faded.

I still clung to a simulacrum of the myth, however, the assumption that a form of success, and on one's own terms, was imminent. Though having discarded those attributes of success I deemed ostentatious (a discarding conveniently performed before acquisition), mentally turning my back on the mansion for a house, the chauffeured limo, the velvet smoking jacket, one perquisite remained for which I could not quell my desire. Some would call it fame; I thought of it as acknowledgement.

Having kept no diary or journal of these halcyon times, I now recall little of day-to-day chronology. Though with clarity I remember my first session creating fiction, I have no idea if this happened the day I moved into my room or two weeks later. I do remember a conversation with a friend named Robert around that time, and the guilt produced by this conversation no doubt precipitated my initial plunge.

Robert and I had met one night at the Mixer's, a quiet bar hidden among industrial buildings east of downtown Minneapolis. It was a place of smoky mirrors and cobwebbed corners, people looming in the background like figures in an Edward Hopper painting. As was becoming our wont, Robert and I talked about writing.

Among my friends, Robert alone encouraged my literary efforts. We were in many ways survivors of an era. The Seventies had decimated our once wide and varied circle of friends, marriage announcements arriving like notices of death. For marriage—more than a house or a job or even a hitch in the service—signified betrayal, a sudden and permanent shift in loyalties. Children were the capstone, the dock to which one's life would be moored. Robert and I had thus far escaped. Indeed, we had stood in shopping malls and openly mocked our less fortunate brothers, those pale excuses for men hurried and harried and harassed by swollen women and squalling replicas.

But these people had something we didn't. They were establishing credit, setting down roots, gaining respectability and (dared we dream it?) self-respect. At least that's the way I eventually saw it. That's the only thing I really envied of my conformist brethren. And now, by writing, I could not only rebel but also "make something of myself," could allay the guilt I had been unable to either acknowledge or ignore.

Tonight, sitting in a high-backed booth, a pitcher of Schmidt between us, Robert told me about a biography of Thomas Wolfe he'd just read, how Wolfe had written while standing up, using the top of a refrigerator for a desk, had literally filled orange crates with manuscript, had been seen one night skipping in the rain, chanting something about having written ten thousand words. The whole point, I gathered, was that Wolfe was a paradigm of intensity, a model for every aspiring writer. I nodded my head and smiled, as if I knew all too well the infernic outpouring that lay ahead. Feeling uncomfortable with the subject—I had yet to write one word intended for publication and had so far felt not the slightest rumbling of any Wolfe-like obsession—I veered the conversation into a different area. Given Robert's predilection for matters literary, why did he himself not write?

Because of the first line, he explained. Robert feared the affliction of Camus' Grand in *The Plague*, writhing like a pinned insect over the opening sentence. There was too much freedom, an infinity of options. Granting the opening sentence importance was natural. The most novice writer senses the advantage of snagging the reader's eye (a gruesome image). But there was also something mystic, Grail-like, about the first line, as if finding that perfect combination of words would unloose a torrent of flawless prose. I disagreed with Robert only in that such a line was unobtainable. Heck, I told him, great opening sentences were popping into my head all the time. My attention span lasting long enough only to marvel at these linguistic gems before wandering down some other path, I thus avoided having to concoct anything past "Sam knew instantly that his neck was broken," viewing what lay beyond that sentence or others like it as a magical and friendly adventure, a pleasant journey beginning as soon as one sat down to business. Though intellectually agreeing with Robert that every writer failed, never saying exactly what he or she wanted, to me this was failure on a grand level, failure to be not avoided but sought.

And so one morning I finally sat down to business. The battleship-grey Underwood rested before me on its cement podium, a sheet of virgin paper round its platen. Originally

19

my grandfather's, the typewriter was less an heirloom than a hand-me-down. I had salvaged it from my cousin's basement where, under the name of "play," the Underwood had suffered untold abuse at the hands of his twin sons; they had even inscribed a bull's eye on its back and shot their BB rifles at it. But the Underwood was a sturdy machine, most likely able to stop bullets much less BBs, and after some cleaning and oiling stood ready to withstand my most passionate assaults.

Following the instructions in *Writer's Market* (a tome invaluable, its own blurbs assured me, to any writer, whether neophyte or professional), I typed my name and address in the upper left corner — this draft was to be my submission! — and in the upper right wrote "Estimated Word Count:," leaving the figure blank; having not yet written the story, I found it difficult to determine its length. Approximately a third of the way down the page, and more or less in the center, I typed "THE CAT KILLER."

Surely such a title would catch the eye of the most passing reader. And what a tale it would be. Content not to write some mere adventure yarn, I would craft a story dripping with symbology — a slayer of cats, an innocent boy, an anarchical future — in short a work that would cause a continental gasp. Having carried the opening line in my head for several days, I now typed it out. And then I paused.

And paused. I felt an unfamiliar pressure; an unseen audience was watching. What was wrong here? I knew well enough in my head what the story was, had described it succinctly to friends, had mulled it to a gem-like perfection while walking or driving or staring out a window. In desperation I typed a second sentence, then a third. By now mentally exhausted, not to mention totally dissatisfied with what was on the paper before me, I put aside the task for a later time.

I began to make the acquaintance of others in the neighborhood. A young married couple lived directly above me, and they were superb arguers. I sat frozen before the Underwood upon first hearing them. Such was the fury of their debate I feared physical violence would ensue, which would mean I'd find out if I had the courage to walk upstairs and intervene. But, much like Ralph and Alice Cramden's grandiose threats (and this argument reminded me of nothing less than a distillation of the loudest and most inane of those *Honeymooner* battles), those of my neighbors were long on style and short on substance.

I ran into them on the landing shortly after this, and we introduced ourselves. Ralph (for so had I dubbed him) was short, squat, muscular, a textbook mesomorph. Lips set in a moist pout, brow furrowed, he exhibited a dangerous combination of intellectual vacuity and insolence. I had the feeling he was sizing me up.

Alice had a more gracious social demeanor, and I could scarce believe it had been she screaming such vulgarities.

She was blonde, taller than Ralph, with features that seemed half-formed, as if an artist had been fearful of finishing delicate work. She was hard and soft, tough-girl pretty, and was, I later discerned, that which helped Ralph survive.

Another duo lived down the street. Homer and C.B. were quintessential drinking buddies, living under a roof provided by the monthly AFDC check of Homer's girlfriend. In their late thirties, they spent much of their time on the front porch (for Homer and C.B. did not work but merely drank) and had developed a Darwinian rivalry with the Salvation Army across the street. Joining them for a beer one afternoon (for they were friendly to passers-by), I watched them in action. As the affluent of society pulled up in their Buicks and Cadillacs, ready to donate their sacks and cardboard boxes of surplus possessions, C.B. would hobble to the street (a hobble up till now nonexistent) and do his best to convince the good people he was as needy as anyone. More often than one would expect, C.B. would return successful. Then it was Christmas. With Homer sitting back on his rocking chair, feet on the porch rail, exhibiting a drunken cockiness reminiscent of Errol Flynn's Robin Hood, C.B. would make a thorough examination of the booty, holding each article up for us to view, trying on the clothes, even the dresses (a ridiculous sight, considering C.B.'s full beard and bald pate). Keeping what they wanted for themselves and friends, C.B. would then stuff the remainder into whatever container it had arrived in, casting it across the street and against the brick wall of the store.

The Salvation Army itself had no lack of characters. On my initial visit, after perusing the threadbare furniture, the rust-pitted kitchen utensils, the two rows of men's suits hanging sad and slouch-shouldered, I descended a wide and musty staircase to the basement. Here lay the flotsam of flotsam, rakes with broken tines, spokeless bicycle rims, decapitated dolls and a thousand other useless items, cascading over tables and chairs and the floor like an unleashed memory. Directly across the room stood, astonishingly, a floor-to-ceiling rack of used books. While perusing these discarded tomes, these high school yearbooks of 1949 and copies of the *Hardy Boys* and *National Velvet*, I made the acquaintance of Little Joe. He had been puttering with something off in a corner but now, upon seeing my interest in the books, made his way to my side, glancing at the staircase as if leery of being spied by a fellow employee. Stoop-shouldered, trembling, eyes watery behind thick spectacles, Joe appeared to be a charity case, banished to "work" in the basement among the quasi-refuse of society.

Ignoring my statement of "just looking," Little Joe took down a book from the third highest shelf, barely within his reach, saying, "Here's something you might be interested in."

It was a copy of *Goldwater, the Man*, the senator's face beaming from the bookjacket. Little Joe turned to the title page. "This is a first edition. Says so right here." The book was held for me to view, to confirm with my own eyes. "It's got to say if it's a first edition," he stated emphatically, as if Congress had recently passed legislation to this effect. I took the book and pretended to be interested, leafing through the pages, realizing that Little Joe had undoubtedly gone through every book on that rack, caring not for the contents or ideas within those pages but only for those two important words. I almost bought the biography but in the end decided against it. How could I take from Joe his secret treasure, this vestige of class in a musty and forgotten basement?

I showed Robert a copy of "The Cat Killer" one night at the Mixer's. He read it right there in the booth. I sat across from him, smoking cigarettes and sipping beer, feigning indifference though in reality aware of Robert's feeblest grunt, his slightest arching of an eyebrow. Upon turning the last page, he said, "We're going places with this one."

Robert's support was sustenance itself. Most of my friends simply looked down at the floor when I mentioned my writing. Those who did speak were inevitably pessimistic, warning of colossal odds and certain defeat. "Why, your chances of making it are about like that," said one, raising his forefinger and thumb, squinting and pretending to create the smallest gap possible. I attributed such predictions to ignorance, not yet acknowledging my own.

Writing the "Cat Killer" was one of the hardest things I'd ever done. I was amazed at the physical difficulty of writing, exhaustion setting in within fifteen minutes or less. Writing was not as I thought it would be, that is it was not simply fitting the appropriate words to one's thoughts, but more like dealing with something alive, like a two-year-old brat, something insisting on its own way and the writer be damned.

Where before I had strolled with ease through that field labeled "spontaneous prose," unencumbered by consideration for tense, punctuation or syntax, I now entered very difficult terrain. Only a basic sense of grammar remained from my twelve years of public education. I remembered that a sentence started with a capital letter and ended with a period; beyond that I had only vague guesses and half-formed theories. Not realizing I had simply to walk three blocks to the library and check out a book on grammar, I began culling a re-education from examples in newspapers and magazines. Spelling was another problem, and again I turned to publications before hitting on the idea of buying a paperback dictionary.

Here it is tempting to portray myself as the young artist obsessed with his vision, a latter-day Martin Eden, eating, sleeping, breathing his craft. In truth, I usually did everything but write before forcing myself to kneel before the Underwood. Much like, after years of a sedentary lifestyle, replete with alcohol, tobacco and deep-fried foods, one takes up jogging and becomes deeply chagrined at collapsing at the quarter-mile mark, I now rued my own errant past. I could sustain concentration for only minutes — sometimes seconds — at a time. I was used to getting up to an alarm clock, to punching a time card, to being told what to do. To summon discipline from within was antithetic to my way of life.

The nickel-and-dime aspects of composition were the most frustrating. Writing as I was—or at least attempting to—a submittable copy, I found my typing skills unequal to the task. Words strayed over the margin, entire clauses would be left out, entire pages rewritten.

But upon completion I felt a pride reminiscent of childhood, of having "done good" at some new and awkward task. I spent a good part of that afternoon pretending to be an editor, repeatedly taking the manuscript out of the manila envelope and trying to read it as though for the first time. This of course had the opposite effect, and eventually the words ceased to evoke any images or cognitions at all. Finally, after one final unreading reading, I inserted a manuscript caked stiff with the pigeon droppings of Correctatype, possessing enough grammatical travesties to make the most seasoned editor howl with laughter, with an opening line of, "The cat knew it was being hunted; knew it, felt it, even there were no overt signs of danger..." into a manila envelope, sealed the flap, and walked down to the mailbox on Nineteenth and Central. An unfamiliar dread filled me as the envelope left my hand. I had shown myself, had dared to dream, to squeal midst the omnipresent clamor.

# 3.

Though my part-time job at the warehouse provided an at least subsistent living (and as a struggling writer I would have had it no other way), it served another purpose as well. My job was, more than anything else, incentive, reminder of a past I wanted nothing more than to flee.

I had worked a variety of jobs over the years—dockworker, foundryman, janitor, bus driver—all of them blue-collar and therefore, despite the plebeian philosophies of my youth, meaningless. One never moved upwards in such a milieu but only horizontally, a process known as "seniority." And seniority scared me. I abandoned these jobs periodically, as though I were striking some weird balance by seeking the freedom of the highway. With each abandonment I vowed never to return to such a life, with its dullness, its insipid tasks, its enervating routine. But of course I did, like a satellite yielding to the earth's pull, reentering the deep, wide and eternally forgiving stratum of the labor market.

My first job out of high school was at the Bigsby Manufacturing Company, a three-story brick factory built before the Union wars. Despite banks of high-powered lathes, glistening key-punches, bright yellow forklifts, the place remained irrepressibly old, as if the opaque and useless windows set forty feet high, the dark corners sunlight had never touched, the dust and dirt and grime, aged all that was young, all that was fresh and alive.

I was trained in by a guy named Smitty. Short and wiry, mid-forties, Smitty had a blunt-featured swarthiness, a kind of New York ugliness, reminiscent of character actors in old movies. Our task was to push a dumpster from lathe to lathe and shovel into it the steel shavings that collected under each machine. The job was slow-paced, and we oft-times stood idle, leaning on our shovels while watching a lathe trough fill up. Occasionally, a twisted strand of metal would fling errant and land on the floor, pulsing red hot in the dust. On one such occasion Smitty looked at me and asked, "What if one of dem hit ya in the pecker? Wouldn't dat hurt?" I could not but shake my head, as if the thought were unbearable. From then on Smitty never missed a chance to comment on the phenomena, asking the same question with each errant strand of steel, to which I would reply with my fatuous headshaking. I remember him as a worried man, laboring midst the legion whine of lathes, pushing his dumpster through columns of dusty sunlight, across cement that replaced earth eight hours a day; and Smitty, working in this machine environment, with its fumes and clamor and tedium, had learned that if a man watched out for anything, it was his pecker. Not that Smitty was the only one with this viewpoint.

Never in my eighteen years had I encountered such an *en masse* preoccupation with libidinous concerns. Sex was everywhere in that dusty clankering building: misspelled graffiti and crude drawings on the lavatory walls, calendars of semi-nude women posing with industrial tools, names and epithets and adjectives all sex-related, fucking-a, cocksucker, motherfucker, asshole, all stated with unflagging enthusiasm.

And yet, despite the constant and harrying reminders of sexuality, these men were surprisingly intolerant of "deviations," of any behavior not in accordance with true manhood. This was brought to light once by a janitor named Jerry, a fat slow-moving man with eyes like a Basset hound's. Sitting with me in the lunchroom one day, Jerry related how a window-washer he knew had happened upon a man and a blonde (women were inevitably relegated to the status of either anatomical parts or hair color) in an upper-story hotel room. "And you know what?" asked Jerry, looking at me from under hirsute eyebrows. I asked what. "The *blonde* was fucking *him,*" he said. I knew what he meant, that the woman had been on top. This unfolding (to me) world of male sexuality had rigid rules indeed!

Oral sex, I learned, was also "deviant," though here rules were more lax. One could admit to having received oral sex, but only via some whore or prostitute, never one's wife or girlfriend. Any reciprocal action was hotly denied — so hotly and so often, in fact, that I began to suspect it was the basis of fantasy for many of the men, that in their heart of hearts they wanted nothing more than to drop to their knees and lap, lap, lap.

And some men, though mouthing the idioms and vulgarities of the shop, seemed strangely sexless, as if years had passed since any stirring in their loins. Baker was one of these. Possessing the body of a Bartlett pear, atop which sat a head so round, so sharp-featured, as to have come off some old Ed Reed *Off the Record* comic strip, Baker also possessed one of the most refined senses of humor I would ever encounter. He had an apparently endless supply of jokes, had in fact introduced himself by way of a joke my first day there, saying, as Smitty and I pushed our dumpster to Baker's lathe, "Hey, kid, didja hear about the old lady who had these two pet monkeys and they both died, and so she took them to the taxidermist, and he said, 'I suppose you want these mounted?' And she said, 'Naw, just holding hands.'" Here Baker did an impression of the old lady, holding his hands together and off to the side, looking up and batting his eyelashes at the imaginary taxidermist, almost blushing for Christ's sake. His timing and erudition had been faultless, and even Smitty — momentarily abandoning his anguish over his pecker — had to laugh.

And there were men who inspired emotions other than mirth. I remember Ollie. Having worked at Bigsby since the goddamn 1930s, Ollie was now treading water till retirement. Stooped and thin, devoid of hair save for a few wisps about his ears, outfitted with oversized and clacking dentures, Ollie's countenance, in the right light, resembled nothing less than a skull draped with skin. Unable to perform any work requiring strength or steadiness, Ollie had been assigned the easiest task in the shop. Daily, he swept out three cavernous and unoccupied rooms on the second floor. I stood back from a door once and watched him, Ollie looking as frail as ever in the expansive and dimly lit room. He could sustain no longer an effort than a dozen swipes of his broom, after which he would lean forward, chest heaving, one skeletal arm dangling like a lightstring. I left quietly. I was eighteen and did not see the irony in the youngest and oldest working the same basic job, how standing in that dusky room, old Ollie and I represented the human fodder of Bigsby Manufacturing and had I cleared my throat or whistled, and had the old man turned, I would have looked not into Ollie's eyes but my own.

# 4.

The arguments overhead veered tack near the end of August. These were hot, muggy, windless days, with surcease from glare and little else when the sun went down. I listened to the arguments nightly, as if they were a radio show, wafting not only through my ceiling but through the open window, bouncing off the brick wall across the alley, backdropped by the sounds of Central Avenue traffic. Where formerly the debates encompassed a variety of subjects, the flirtatious glance Ralph had given some waitress or Alice squeezing toothpaste from the middle of the tube, they now centered exclusively on one matter: Ralph finding a job.

Alice was pregnant, and don't think she was about to live with a man who wouldn't support his own family, his own flesh and blood. Didn't Ralph understand that pretty soon she wouldn't be able to work? And then what? How were they going to pay the bills? The rent? And what was the baby going to eat?

Ralph, to his credit, never argued that he shouldn't work, only that jobs were pretty darn hard to come by and don't tell him he wasn't looking. It wasn't his fault unemployment was so high. He wasn't running the goddamn government.

Perhaps Ralph did look for work, though such could not be proven by my testimony. He began to visit me daily, waiting till Alice had left for her nursing home job before knocking on my door. At first these visits were on some pretext or other, the old cup-of-sugar routine, developing all too quickly into regular and informal "chats," Ralph sitting without being asked, placing his feet on my orange-crate coffee table, asking if I had any beer. Conversations with Ralph tended to be one-sided, little more than recitations of his numerous and, if nothing else, imaginative adventures. I put up with this at first, fascinated by the pathological liar before me. Ralph routinely beat up entire motorcycle gangs, saved people from drowning, outraced squad cars, and a plethora of other episodes gleaned, I suspected, more from television than from life.

Soon these "conversations" became dotted with references such as "friends like us" or "buddies like you and me" till one day I listened in horror as Ralph disclosed that I was his best friend. Lacking the courage to simply tell him to fuck off, which would have been the sanest approach, I began coming up with my own imaginative excuses why he could not bend my ear. The most used was that I had to write. On first hearing this, Ralph looked askance at me, but I made sure to type after he left so he could hear me from his apartment. This daily clacking, combined with the increasingly numerous piles of manuscript surrounding the beanbag and cement podium, eventually convinced Ralph I was indeed a writer.

Ralph and Alice were a loony couple, augmenting Alice's minimum-wage income with third-rate scams — switching price tags at department stores, stealing rolls of toilet paper from public restrooms, shoplifting at garage sales. Probably because I was a decade older, not to mention a "writer," they placed on my shoulders a sage-like wisdom, seeking my advice on overdue bills, job applications and other "brainy stuff." In turn, I was invited to their apartment every two weeks or so for dinner.

31

I began to kneel before my typewriter with something less than glee. Nothing seemed good, every combination of words but a pitiable attempt at coherency. Rather than forming a cohesive plan, or even a vague outline, I simply waited for inspiration to sweep over me, washing away such mundane requirements as plot, structure, revision. I wrote now only out of guilt. I have kept writing these past years for many reasons, but the unwavering motivation, that which stood while all others crumbled, has been guilt.

One evening at the Mixer's, Robert, with acumen I marvel at to this day, causing me to suspect he was actually an editor on some primal level, a Maxwell Perkins in the rough, hit on the reason for my recent sputtering: "You've got to stop thinking about the *Playboy* story. Just decide on another one and start working on it."

Though simple enough advice, it was perfectly apt. My frustration was due in no small way to the "Cat Killer's" unknown fate, as if the manuscript had sucked my energy along its postal orbits. I had not bothered to note the date of submission and therefore had no way of knowing how long the story had been out. Surely it had been longer than the two to three weeks listed in *Writer's Market*. A heretofore dormant superstition crept into my life. I discerned omens in the most trivial of events, an overheard conversation, a honking horn, a cloud passing before the sun. Not to mention the manufactured omens. Landing a crumpled piece of paper in the wastebasket at the far end of the room meant the story would be accepted; the same for jabbing the end of a lightstring three consecutive times; and a dozen other modern-day versions of entrails-casting — all geared to betoken success.

But I could not stave self-doubt. What qualifications had I to be a writer? Possessing a marginal high school education, and but fifty minutes of a college, I had taken but one writing course my entire life, and that lasted two days.

This was during my senior year of high school. Desiring to make these last nine months of enforced education (for unlike my peers I had no plans to attend college) as nontaxing as possible, I had, as much as the curriculum would allow, opted for the "easy" classes — Russian history, intramural sports, wood shop, and, for reasons having long since escaped the pull of memory, Creative Writing One.

My mistake was apparent the first minute of the first day. The teacher was a wizened despot named Mrs. Wagg, and, as she eyed our class for several seconds after the bell rang, much in the manner I would in later years see drill sergeants eye fresh recruits, I experienced an urge to flee. After her surveillance, in which her wrinkled face betrayed no emotion other than disdain, Mrs. Wagg removed her cat's-eye glasses and with an Ethel Merman authority introduced herself. She then strode through the aisles, high heels tapping methodic progress as she opined on subjects more or less related to writing. This was done in a pedantic monotone, as if Mrs. Wagg were bored by the whole matter, this dispensing of wisdom, but was bound by her contractual commitment. Eventually, a good three-quarters of the hour spent, Mrs. Wagg gave us our first assignment: to spend the remainder of the time writing whatever we wanted.

As we furrowed our brows and nibbled our pencils, Mrs. Wagg, like some stiletto-heeled Ahab, continued to stride the aisles. Occasionally pausing, she would take a student's paper, arch her eyebrows, and scan the primal inedita, the classroom a sea of silence. Making a comment or two — plainly audible — Mrs. Wagg would hand the paper back and continue on her way. Eventually, as I had feared, Mrs. Wagg stopped at my desk.

Having elected to write about a dog my family owned years ago, I had inscribed no more than two sentences upon suffering my first critique. "It is obvious from this," said Mrs. Wagg, "that you are a dog lover."

The next day was even worse. Again, three-quarters of an hour was consumed by Mrs. Wagg's pontifications. Though I remember little of what was said, my ears performing that sanity-saving function common to all students and closing their inner lids, I recall one statement with clarity. Mrs. Wagg had wound her way to the subject of Ernest Hemingway, discoursing not on his work but on the man himself. "Hemingway wrote in the *Old Man and the Sea* that 'a man can be destroyed but never defeated,'" she said, "an axiom he himself disproved by committing suicide in 1961."

What galled me most was not Mrs. Wagg's arrogant assumption, her dismissal of Hemingway's final act as defeat, but my own inability to articulate an objection, an inability fostered not only by the institution we both served but from some innate part of myself. I transferred into a study hall the next day.

Now, kneeling in my "garret" in northeast Minneapolis, I wondered if I had acted wisely. Could Mrs. Wagg have taught what I was now trying to learn? Or would such a path been suicidal, like Mrs. Wagg's appraisal of Hemingway, a quick and sure descension into defeat?

The story returned. I had almost given up on it, mentally composing a letter of inquiry to *Playboy* upon each daily no-show, the "letter" growing evermore biting and vehement. As it was, the manuscript's presence took me by surprise, as if the whole episode had been but a particularly vivid fantasy. Yet there it was, doubled lengthwise, jutting out the top of my brass mailslot. I hardly dared touch it.

That a magazine would not return a purchased manuscript had yet to occur to me, and I indulged in the mystery of the sealed envelope. I held it up to the light, as if the manila paper had grown translucent during its voyage. I hefted it, smelled it, placed it on the orange-crate coffee table and tried not to think about it. Finally, much as a child

34

opening the last Christmas present, that which could salvage his morning of anticipation or plunge it into despair, I tore open the envelope and removed its contents.

Paperclipped to the first page was a small memo sheet. Near the top of the sheet was the famous rabbit's head, beneath was a succinct, marginally polite rejection.

And that was that. A study in anticlimax. I'd spent weeks writing the story, twice that long waiting for a reply. The manuscript had logged eight-hundred miles to Chicago and back, had been dropped on someone's desk, handled, opened, and—if even for a moment, that moment before those first few words were read—considered for publication. Ultimately to return, to sit on my orange crate.

I reread the story, embarrassed at the outlandish similes, the laughable dialogue, the splotches of Correcta-type. These faults I could see. But to discern the heart of the problem , the secret that would shape this mangled prose into good prose, was to peer into the dark and wavering form of mystery itself.

# 5.

On a cold morning in early October I found myself sitting on a leather couch in a suburban living room, listening to a man and woman I had yet to meet argue hysterically behind a bathroom door. The episode was a turning point in many ways.

Fall had come gently that year, with skies of blue chalk and solar warmth. Evenings were balmy, perfect for sitting on the front stoop of Mrs. McAdam's building, drinking beer, watching people and cars. Though I still wrote daily, a seasonal sap had entered my body, a loss of intensity corresponding to the sun arcing ever lower on the horizon. Sessions with the Underwood were brief, cap shots of inspiration. Ostensibly working on my next submission, the fated *Omni* story, I turned to this task with but loathing, preferring instead the intriguing description, the clever sentence that led nowhere. Only occasionally did I attend to the nuts and bolts of true composition, and then with but plodding, oxen progress.

Other matters began to fill my time. The reader may have by now noticed, in this tale, a lack of romance. Embarking on my literary quest, my quixotic assault on the windmills of publishing, I had taken a quasi-vow of, if not outright celibacy, then at least noninvolvement. I was twenty-nine years old, and I knew by now that you didn't get something for nothing. With the warmth of a body, the availability of sex, the guarantee of companionship, came an increase in social outings (few women regarded bar-hopping as cultural), shopping forays, a whole new set of friends and relatives. I could ill-afford these distractions. For now, my role—barring of course the odd hedonistic fling—would be that of the solitary, celibate artist.

But this decision had been made with the asinine enthusiasm heralding the start of any journey, metaphorical or real. Now, as the nights came quicker and stayed longer, as I climbed between cold and unwashed sheets and huddled fetus-like for warmth, a vague loneliness entered my body. Despite my resolve, I began to crave, even more than sex, companionship.

Enter Maria. I first saw her one night at Momart's. She was sitting at a table near the door, drinking black coffee, periodically glancing out the window and at her watch. A silken mass of black hair draped past her shoulders, framing classic, aquiline features, eyes like glistening coal. She sat ignored by the other patrons, as if Momart's whitewashed walls and sawdust floor rendered such exoticness invisible. More out of curiosity than anything, I moved near her and struck a conversation.

Maria was from Brazil, attending the university via a student-exchange program. Having finished a night class of English at the local high school, she was now waiting for a bus. And what did I do? Well, I guess you could say I was a writer. Oh really?

And just like that we were seeing each other. Gone was my determination to remain uninvolved, to channel carnal energy into writing. I would wait for Maria outside Edison High School every Tuesday and Thursday night, leaning my back against the cold brick wall, smoking Pall Malls. Then the doors opened and the "students" would straggle out.

Maria was the only one who really looked like a student. The others were older, apparently immigrants, Asians in over-sized stocking caps, East Europeans with trench coats and somber eyes. Maria would link her arm with mine, and we would walk through nights of dwindling warmth, Maria recounting what she had learned that evening, the consonants, the vowels, the spelling, the struggle. Sometimes we would stop at Momart's or the Crest Cafe or the Ideal Diner for coffee and talk through the falling of the night, our own intimate patois of English, Portuguese and *amor*.

Maria lived with a sponsor family in the southern suburbs. Judging from her descriptions, Maria's adoptive family may well have stepped out of a Norman Rockwell painting: Mother, Father, two blonde and apple-cheeked daughters, all white as alabaster, as wholesome as six-grain bread. Not that they were untainted by preconception. The mother, apparently, did not think highly of me, warning Maria that I was "no good." That Mother concluded this without having met me (I had visions of her parting the curtains of some upper-bedroom window as I walked from my eyesore of a truck to their linen-white front door) was not cause for offense. I had done the same, had preformed my own opinions, desiring as much as she that our paths remained uncrossed.

Maria appended her disclosure with "But no one tells me what to do." Indeed, few people did. But what had first seemed an admirable, feline independence in Maria developed quickly into a sweet-scented domination. As the days grew shorter, the leaves more vibrant, the sun less warm, I found *my* time becoming *our* time, that it was easier to go along with Maria's scheduling than to kneel before the Underwood. Allowing this to happen meant I lacked resolve; resenting and blaming Maria meant I lacked courage to face my own shortcomings.

Events came to a head one cold Saturday morning. Opening the linen-white door, Maria informed me our plans, that of shopping and an afternoon movie, were changed. Her friend Peppe, another exchange student, was going to meet us here at the house, from whence we would go out for lunch. For the first time since I had known her, Maria bade me enter the suburban abode.

The door opened onto the kitchen. Two tow-headed girls sat at the kitchen table, spooning cereal into their mouths while watching a small black-and white television atop a breadbox. We sidled past them—the girls affording me not the slightest acknowledgement—and into the living room. Apparently today was laundry day. Piles of socks and underwear, pajamas and towels and jeans and tee-shirts, were strewn across the taupe carpet, the leather couch, the glass-topped coffee table. Maria moved a pile of sheets and we sat on the couch.

What had at first seemed a loud muffled conversation from some indeterminate part of the house was now recognizable as a full-blown argument. Obviously Mother and Father were having a spat. Pointing down the hall whence the argument came, I told Maria we should leave before they came out and discovered us, or, more accurately, me. No, she said, Peppe was on her way and we had to wait. I suggested we wait outside. No, it was too cold. Maria linked her arm through mine and sat back. She had commented more than once on the casual and commonplace violence in America, no doubt considering a bathroom argument little cause for embarrassment.

Seconds ticked by, Maria and I sitting in the livingroom, the daughters ingesting their cartoon meal, the argument escalating beyond all degrees of propriety. It was, in fact, becoming one-sided. Mother had gained the upper hand, her voice rising to that of a termagant's—punctuated infrequently by a pitiable male voice—until reaching an inhuman shrillness, a banshee tongue-lashing that to this day I thank God was not directed at me. Fearing this signaled the end (Mother was bound to grow hoarse if nothing else), I held an imaginary phone to my ear and pointed to the kitchen, telling Maria to call Peppe's sponsor home and see if she had left. But she was soon to arrive, said Maria. "Just call and see," I insisted.

Three things then happened: Maria rose to make her phone call, I allowed myself to relax, and the argument abruptly ceased, a gunshot silence in the air. I heard the slapping of bare feet, and Mother strode into view. Clad in a dark-blue bathrobe (the writer's curse, I was noting detail even now), her hair wet and stringy, Mother stopped at the end of the hall, leaning forward while furiously drying her hair with a towel. Wrapping the towel turban-like round her head, she snapped upright and saw me.

There was a moment of shock, a wordless vacuum in which we were both suspended. A brittle truce formed, and through a mask of china Mother said:

"Hello."

All the unwelcomeness, scorn and out-and-out detestation possible had been squeezed into the word. I could but point spinelessly at Maria, saying, "She's trying to call some friends." Replying with not one word or gesture, as if, like that of a cockroach's or slug's, Mother had acknowledged my presence, the basic fact of my existence, and nothing more, she spun on her heel and strode back down the hallway. A door slammed shut.

Would that the tale ended there. Maria motioned the phone at me: "She wants to talk to you." I took the phone. A woman's voice, all throaty and vampy hoarse, like some aged actress who'd sucked down three packs of Camel straights for forty years, identified itself as Peppe's sponsor mother. (Where do they find these families?) Apologizing for having difficulty understanding Maria, the voice explained that

Peppe had left to meet us at a local shopping center. I said I wished I had known that five minutes ago.

"Are you mad?" asked the voice.

I said that yes, I supposed I was mad. I could hear a cigarette being lit, a breathy pause, and then, "Well, what are you?" Assuming she hadn't heard me, I reiterated that I was mad. But no, no, she didn't mean that.

"What *are* you?" she asked, then in a tone of pointing out the obvious, said, "You're a *man*, aren't you?"

What did she expect me to do? Sock Maria in the jaw? A decade or two earlier I could have answered, yes, damn it, I was a man, and pursued whatever bulldog path lay before me. But I was a product of the Seventies, swathed in the effeminacy of the "new man." I "understood," tried to be "fair," believed in "equality." I had no desire for vengeance, for righting wrongs that may or may not have transpired that morning. I wanted only to escape. I told the voice that, yes, I was a man, thanked it for its help, and hung up.

Viewing the episode as an omen, a foretoken of what lay waiting on my current path—I did not want to wind up a husband in the bathroom—I returned to writing with a vengeance, seeing less and less of Maria till she showed up at the front door of Mrs. McAdam's building one night in late November, the sky black and grey-ragged behind her. She said everything she had to say, why didn't I call her, what was the matter, and she couldn't really stay but had to catch a bus, and I knew she was hinting for a ride but I let her walk off, thus not ending the affair cleanly, like a "man," but cowardly, like putting off going to the dentist until finally the pain goes away and you don't feel it no more.

# 6.

The *Omni* story was my first attempt at science-fiction. Though possessing all the scientific knowledge of a nineteenth century Watusi, I reckoned this a minor impediment. I had steeped myself in the genre during my high school days, staving off blackboard ennui by fighting alongside John Carter of Mars, soaring with Heinlen's pubescent space cadets, marveling at Asimov's all-too-human robots. Now, standing in Wajik's drugstore, skimming the stories of Analog and Fantasy and Weird Tales, comparing those sorry attempts with my own work-in-progress, I felt as confident describing flying pterodactyls and laser beams as anyone.

There were several magazines to aim for, though most of them were of diminutive size and pay scale, printed on what appeared to be erased grade school paper. But *Omni* was large and slick, splashed with color, the *Playboy* of the science market—and paid five times what the lesser rags doled out.

The plot, again the least of my problems, employed a concept dating to H.G. Wells—time travel. What if? What if someone went back in time and supplied his future parents with stock market reports, real estate values, football scores? That person would be born rich, that's what. Assuming that science fiction needed a moral, some heavy-handed lesson bludgeoned into the reader, I devised an O. Henry ending, or at least what I viewed as such an ending. The parents, exulting in their new-found wealth and not wishing to be burdened with children, would procure an abortion, thus the time traveler being the originator of his own destruction.

Now all I had to do was write the damn thing. It was a putrid attempt. Impatience was my master, inability my foe. The parents resided in a furnitureless house, possessed faces devoid of features, the time traveler seemed "oddly familiar." But I was writing, oblivious to these and many other shortcomings, and I felt oddly content.

I received a letter from my mother around this time. This surprised me. My mother had an eye-for-an-eye attitude about letters, Christmas cards, thank-you notes and such, and I had owed her for weeks. Despite my professed avocation, and for reasons not easily defined, I detested writing letters, putting off such tasks until overpowered by guilt. Recognizing my mother's lean graceful script, I felt a pang of homesickness:

Dear Harrison:

We've been expecting to hear from you! I think you need a phone — at least we could call you. Hope you're okay and doing good at work. Did you get that raise?

All is fine here. The weather's been real good. If only July and August weren't so hot, Arkansas would have perfect weather. But you can't have everything!

We enjoyed your last letter, but I had to read the first page twice before I got it. Maybe it would be better if you simmered down a little.

People have to be able to read what you write, you know.

Well, not much news. Call your cousin more often, and Es and Jim, Alma and Chet, so they know you're okay. Write soon and send us some of your stories. I'm anxious to read them!

Love,
Mom and Dad

The reference to my last letter made me wince. My parents, while not flat-out opposed to my writing, did not number among my most ardent supporters. More than once they suggested I settle down (meaning the procurement of job, wife and house payments) and then write in my "spare time." Wanting to prove my mettle, to win my parents over (and does one ever outgrow this?), I had sent them great longwinded epistles, pages of grammatical acrobatics, logorrheic verbiage, obscure and wrongly used words, all but unreadable or, as my mother mentioned, having to be "read twice."

The letter affected me in other ways, too. My earlier use of the word "homesickness" was telling. My home, meaning the land I mostly grew up in, was right here. But my parents had retired a few years ago and moved to rural Arkansas, and in a sense home had moved with them.

Family was important to my mother, and her request that I keep in touch with my cousin and other relatives, her long-distance attempt to hold together an increasingly incohesive unit, was poignant. A week earlier I had run into an uncle at an all-night restaurant, and had learned the erosion of family came not so much from time and death but from personality, choices made, paths taken.

I hadn't seen Uncle Eddie since my grandfather's funeral three years ago. Married and divorced an indeterminate number of times and generally adhering to a sybaritic lifestyle, Uncle Eddie was the closest our family had to a black sheep. Reunions were held in his absence, as were familial observances of holidays, weddings, birthdays, though, as if in the face of cosmic darkness human pettiness was abandoned, Uncle Eddie did attend funerals. Sitting in the restaurant with him now, I found the person before me did not jibe with memory, the salt-and-pepper hair and loose-fleshed countenance were not those of the tall skinny guy who took me for fast rides and bought me cherry Cokes.

We went out drinking the next night, Uncle Eddie, like days of old, supplying transportation with his new car. A succession of salesman jobs had kept Uncle Eddie in varying degrees of solvency over the years, and he had become an expert at financed splendor, mortgaging happiness against the payments on his Cadillac and the size of his bar tab. To watch him that evening was to see a catalogue of emotions. Starting out, Uncle Eddie was jubilant, swilling an everpresent grapefruit juice and vodka, slapping backs, dancing with sometimes real, sometimes imaginary women. We changed scenery often, each ride more swerving and hilarious than the last. Eventually, we wound up in some country-western bar on the northern outskirts of town, the table between us sloppy with spilled beer and melted ice, the evening almost spent. Uncle Eddie descended into a profound silence, staring at some spot two feet above the floor, his lips moving slightly. Then he began to unburden himself, a slow thick unburdening, a recounting of sins past and irredeemable, of family quarrels, lost jobs, failed marriages, of a barroom life and the awful vacuum of Sunday morning. Finally, leaning his elbows on the sotted table, Uncle Eddie held his palms as if in supplication and bade me look.

"See these hands?" he asked. "These hands ain't never had a callous on 'em. I make my living with my mouth, and that's all I fucking got."

A pervasive depression enveloped me after this. Loss of family, loss of love, every loss conceivable, haunted my thoughts at all hours, whether working, writing, walking. But the depression was most intense late at night, when I would slide between cold and unwashed sheets, the world outside small and dark, and I realized we are born alone and except for rare and sparkling moments we live alone, the steely shard of cynicism everpresent and addicting, forgiveness rare, strangers on streets, meandering paths, killing time before death, and strangers all, buy me a drink, Uncle Eddie?

# 7.

The dinners Ralph and Alice invited me up for were always great, old-fashioned meals, pork chops or rump roast or fried chicken, mashed potatoes, green beans and bacon — welcome relief from my diet of fried-egg sandwiches and instant coffee. After dinner we would sit around the table, drinking coffee, smoking cigarettes, listening to Ralph's outlandish tales. I had begun to enjoy these recitations in a perverse sort of way, viewing them more as entertainment than any assault on my credulity.

But one night Alice held the floor, going on about their forthcoming child — Alice was six months along — and the procurement of baby paraphernalia. Their apartment was more crammed with stuff every time I saw it, oversized boxes of Pampers, a playpen, rattles and mobiles, cardboard boxes of used shirts and pants and bibs donated by friends and relatives; a white crib stood in what had been Ralph's weightlifting room. Up till now Ralph had been sitting with a vacuous stare on his face, lips in a moist pout. I realized Ralph was already jealous of the baby. As if my thoughts tripped a signal, Ralph suddenly interrupted Alice. "Aw, shut up, pig. Who wants to listen to your fat mouth?"

Ralph went on, berating Alice for "letting herself go," as if pregnant women should somehow maintain slim figures.

Not wishing to be caught, literally, in the middle of one of their fights, I attempted to defuse the situation, offering the observation that Alice's was not a permanent condition.

"Permanent condition," echoed Ralph. "Listen to the professor."

Later that night, kneeling before the Underwood, I found myself thinking about Ralph's reaction. Was such a phrase really outside his ken? I had once worked in a foundry in North St. Paul with a man named Gerald. Despite the baseness of our surroundings, the squalor typical of the bottom rung of American plebeianism, Gerald acted and spoke in a donwright scholarly manner, clearing his throat before speaking, prefacing sentences with appositives and other premeditative phrases, even using (he once confided to me) parenthetical insertions. For Gerald a certain task was not a "pain in the ass" but "possessed of a significant amount of deterrents"; the secretary in the office was not a "stone fox" but one who was "pulchritudinous." The other men, at first bewildered and bemused by this bird, soon began to mock him openly, eventually forcing Gerald into a sustained silence. Was I, despite my professed sympathies, driving away from my very goal, that of communication?

My latest written attempt at communication was now finished. Forcing out the last page of the third draft late one night, I vowed it the hardest work I'd ever done. I was reluctant to bid it farewell, this second professional submission, the manuscript in a "polished" state. In truth, it was even worse than the first story, possessing not only its share of splotched corrections and words spilling past the margin line but also two pages on which I had inserted carbon paper backwards, as though the prose had seared completely through the paper. The prose itself (I say in hindsight) was slightly more lucid. I was emulative of Hemingway's simplistic style, or at least what I took to be such a style. Sentences were short, description nonexistent.

The point of view was promiscuous, bedding down with whatever characters presented themselves. But by what standard could I judge it?

Much in the grim nervous manner one buries one's dead, I sheathed the manuscript, sealed it, donned my late grandfather's greatcoat, and walked down to the mailbox on Central Avenue. I released the envelope with but a trace of hesitation.

I went for a walk. In the incognizant way one recovers from a cold or headache, realizing that at some forgotten point the ailment had vanished, I now found my depression similarly departed. Or, rather, it had been replaced by a more wholesome melancholy, the melancholy of fall.

I have always liked cloudy days, trees without leaves, solitary birds. The sadness of fall was one I had long ago come to terms with, had, even, grown to love. A decade ago I had been in Fort Leonardwood, Missouri, awaiting a medical discharge from the army. Since such a process takes weeks, I was assigned a superfluous job in a supply room, entailing chores no more strenuous than walking to the PX to buy Marlboros for the staff sergeant. My evenings and weekends were free, and, tired of swilling watery beer in the enlisted men's clubs, listening to the obscene and monosyllabic utterances that passed for conversation in such places, I chanced one night to discover the base library and, in a larger sense, rediscover books. The weather, up till then a blue-skied, gold-tinged elongation of summer, now turned misty and grey, days of drizzle, nights of thunder. I read Poe. Night after night, sitting on a vinyl couch in the reading area, heavenly mortar flashing outside the plate-glass windows, I experienced the rhythmic terror of "The Raven," the progressive dissolution of "The Tell-Tale Heart." Entranced by Poe's mastery, I felt anew the power of the written word, and to Poe I owe this debt.

Though the library owned several collections of his work, the one I preferred was a threadbare, brown-jacketed volume, its pages thick and smooth. I never checked the book out, returning it to its shelf at closing time and trusting to fate it would be there on the morrow. I would then walk the gravel roads back to my barracks, the sky spent with lightning, rain slashing down in hesitant sweeps, words fresh aboil and quothe the raven nevermore.

# BOOK TWO

# THE DELETION OF
# UNNECESSARY WORDS

# 1.

It is time to speak of the road. Three days before Christmas I found myself standing on the southbound shoulder of Interstate 35W, bound with thumb and backpack for my parents' home in Arkansas. A half-dozen rides had placed me fifty miles south of the Twin Cities, there to stand in frozen farmland, the sun well into its afternoon descent, the traffic sparse. I thought seriously of turning back.

Though having once embraced the myth of the road, the comforting nihilism epitomized by Kerouac and Cassady, I was now possessed of a guarded disillusionment. Unlike the vagabonds I admired and wanted nothing more than to emulate—Kerouac, London, Guthrie—I was lousy at being "on the road." My excursions were distressingly prosaic. I never toiled alongside migrant workers, was never shot at, never discovered beautiful and willing women in my sleeping bag. Even my arrest in a small town in Utah had been an understated affair, the policemen acting quiet and self-conscious, nearly apologetic.

Despite realizing life does not conform to celluloid images or words within a book (truly some of my most miserable days have been spent on the road), I found much about traveling appealing, the shedding of habits and routines and familiar sights, the simplification of one's life. Motion itself was compelling, destination dwindling to secondary importance.

And to travel was to have a goal, a reason for existence, a ticket into realms more primal, more sweeping.

My decision to hitchhike, however, was based more on economics than any thirst for adventure. The plant I worked at had closed down two weeks for Christmas, and I had not decided till this morning whether to leave or spend my hiatus writing. Had I not recently finished the Omni story, I likely would have remained in Minneapolis. My liquid assets totaling less than thirteen dollars, I could travel only via the charity of others, a Brahmin of the American highways.

Having never hitchhiked this long a distance, I spent a good deal of the morning stalling, pacing the apartment and smoking cigarettes, trying to think of what else to stuff into my backpack. Ralph stopped down and, upon hearing my plans, asked with brutish candor if I knew what I was doing. Though answering cavalierly — "No, but that never stopped me before" — I was unable to prevent Ralph's query from intensifying my fears. Weather forecasts coming over my alarm clock radio warned of a cold front moving in, of temperatures dropping to six-below. Chiding myself for gutlessnes — I could be well to the south before nightfall — I shouldered my pack, locked my door, and walked down to the Johnson Street entrance ramp.

This trip was laden with prodigal implications. My father hailed from central Arkansas, and family vacations had been spent riding whatever Pontiac we owned at the time (seemingly all men of that era swore allegiance to the various strains of Detroit iron, my father being a "Pontiac man") south on U.S. 65, passing through Des Moines, Springfield, Harrisonville. Normally short-tempered and brusque, upon taking command of the Bonneville (for he was not only a Pontiac man but a Bonneville man), my father became gradually quieted, leaning forward, muscular forearms draped across the steering wheel, as if contentment were in ratio to the miles consumed by the expansive hood. My mother, the familial co-pilot, sat next to him, lighting his Camels, pouring coffee, dispensing gum and sandwiches and bottles of pop. My brother and I rode in the back midst pillows and comic books and magnetic checkerboards, and sometimes, during barreling lulls across Iowa, or descending the curves of the Ozarks, I would position myself so as to catch my father's reflection in the rearview mirror, his eyebrows and hazel irises framed by plastic trim. I would covertly study this image, as if it were an animal captured, something to be examined and then, with a child's discretion, either destroyed or set free.

Such a trip was always the main event of summer vacation. Taking a child's delight in riding anywhere, to school or church or a relative's house, my sense of adventure was heightened by entering a land that was different, the vegetation threateningly verdant, radio voices increasingly nasal. We read Burma-shave signs, pleaded with Father to stop at Dogpatch, U.S.A., spent long minutes staring out the rear window at where we'd been. Waitresses and gas station attendants moved slowly, were astonishingly polite. And the land was different in other ways. At a gas station in Arkansas I asked my father why they had a restroom marked "colored people." Busy paying the attendant, my father did not answer me but instead smiled at the other man, explaining that I was from "up north."

Though my father drove heedless of rain, fog, or belly of night, pushing the Pontiac till the rest of us fell asleep (secure with Father at the wheel), upon reaching his parents' house he would immediately want to leave, to recover the ground we had spent the last two days barreling across. A kind of bragging suffused this impatience.

Prior to our arrival, my father inevitably stopped at a smokehouse and bought a large ham, which my brother and I would present to our grandparents. It was as if my father were saying, with the ham, the late-model Pontiac, the pretty wife and healthy kids, that he was not only surviving but surviving quite well, thank you. And part of this northern success was to display impatience. My memory is that of a man standing awkwardly in wallpapered rooms, as if they were garments outgrown, jingling keys in his pocket, citing reasons for returning north in undue haste. The whole process was a mystery to me, this prodigal and moth-like obligation of my father's, this urge that came from within and once appeased held no more power.

My grandparents lived in a small town in central Arkansas. Enola ("alone" spelled backwards) was little more than buildings clustered around a crossroads, a Mobile gas station, post office, Murphy's general store. Each house lining County Highway 22, or "main street" as it was known between the backs of the speed limit signs, had a barn behind it, and an outhouse, and a well with a hand pump. Beyond the barns were fields, and beyond those, scrubby vegetation and concealing woods.

Once a day my brother and I would walk to Murphy's store, stepping past the old men sitting on the porch on wooden chairs and on the Diamond Feed Mill's bench. These men were there all day, all but motionless, watching the passage of cars and slinking dogs and children sent on errands. They fascinated me, these men with dusty coveralls and plaid shirts (in this heat!), their hands clasped atop hickory sticks, their squinting eyes, their subtle and inexplicable embarrassment in our presence. My brother and I would walk past them into the big, high-ceilinged store, stepping into cavern coolness, ceiling fans in lazy propellation, even flies were lazy down here, depositing a dime into the Coca-cola cooler, opening the lid and feeling the cold air through our tee-shirts, selecting a bottle of grape or orange or, usually, Coke, grabbing it by its neck and working it through the sheetmetal maze of the cooler, other bottles tinkling like wind chimes. Why did those old men sit there? No one sits there now.

Nights were magic in Enola. We would sit on the front porch, Grandpa and Grandma in the swing, aunts and uncles in love seats and creaking rockers, cousins—the young'uns—sitting on the edge of the porch or running into the blackness after fireflies. And Grandpa would tell stories. He was a craggy-faced laconic man during the day, but in the softness of the night he became a voice, carried on an oral tradition. These were great stories, autobiographical, unhurried, detailed, sometimes seedy, one of the family occasionally interrupting to make a point or bring up a part that had been skipped (for these stories were oft-repeated, being requested much like songs at a piano bar). I loved these nights. Nothing like them existed up north. Up there families were already spending evenings in front of television screens, listening to stories told by people they didn't know, stories they could not interrupt or clarify, stories heralded by Fruit Loops and finished by Noxzema shaving cream. And by now the South had joined the North, had abandoned the best literary tradition it had, the porches dark and unused, the fireflies shining unmolested.

Upon retirement my father fulfilled a decades-old vow (emphatically resworn every Minnesota winter) and, along with my mother and her poodle and their household furnishings, moved back to the town he had left as a young man, to what had over the years assumed the stature of a Xanadu. That I was following a well-trod path did not escape me, though comparisons could be made on but the most basic levels. I was not driving a family car on summer vacation but was fleeing south in the dead of winter, would arrive not successful but nearly broke, and only in the most temporal sense would I be returning "home."

# 2.

As the sun touched the horizon—that rolling, snow-covered, farmland horizon—a baby-blue Chevette pulled over. The driver was a college student on his way home to Omaha, which for me meant passage all the way to Des Moines. The kid was thin, with long hair parted in the middle, wire-rimmed glasses atop a beakish nose. A white plastic crucifix hung from the rearview mirror.

We talked for half an hour or so, a general conversation about the unseasonably warm weather, the Minnesota Vikings, Jimmy Carter's chances of reelection. And then the kid made the noises of proselytizing. He started by relating his life history. I remember no details, just a monotonic recitation of an aimless life, void of meaning, replete with temptation— here a confession of "dabbling in drugs"—transformed suddenly into a full life, a reborn happiness whether rising, sleeping or eating. And had I, he asked, ever considered taking Jesus into my heart?

What a setting! Hurtling down the highway, patches of snow on fallow land, cornstalks like dead sentinels, a fading sunset to the right, blackness to the left, a thin young man asking me to accept Jesus.

There were many points I could have argued, *had* argued in years past, but I no longer had the heart for such debate. My irreligousness peaked during my "college years." Back then I was eager not so much to understand the world as explain it, to encase it within the boundaries of my own meager scope. One way to do this was through cynicism. Television was an easy and available target (though my friends and I were never so cynical as to turn the damn thing off), and late-night television, with its plethora of B-westerns and oft-repeated sitcoms, of spastic car salesmen, was the easiest target of all. The last show at night was "Pastor Hammond's Sermonette," and we had developed a ritual around it. Two plaster figurines of Jesus — one blackfaced with magic-marker in the name of collegiate fair play — stood atop the television; as the strains of "Onward Christian Soldiers" emitted from the tinny speaker, we would march the figurines down the sides of the set (much like Wolfe's Piggy Logan and his traveling circus), standing them before the screen as Pastor Hammond delivered his abbreviated yet intense sermon. I can still see them staring up at the grainy image, their hands in supplication, their figures hued neon. I was twenty-two years old, and if I could not explain, I would mock.

I was now facing thirty and had learned that a container holding acid could also be eaten by it, that explanations, short-lived and fragile though they may be, are not to be flippantly dismissed. I did not want to take from this young man, by clever and logical argumentation, by questioning how "aimless" one's life can be at nineteen, any belief he found comforting. I dealt with him forthright, saying I was not interested in being saved nor did I care to discuss it. Not to be dissuaded, the kid lowered his voice and in a confidential tone, as though I would be incapable of believing what I was about to hear, said, "You know, I prayed before I left that I'd be able to pick up a hitchhiker and share the Lord with him."

Apparently an adherent of gentle persuasion, the kid let the issue drop. He had done his part, had presented me with the key to salvation; that I declined was not his fault. We drove into the night. I stared out the window for long stretches, the Iowa countryside hidden and deep, black land under black night, and I tried to deal with the thoughts and memories our conversation had unloosed.

The situation reminded me of a car trip I'd taken years earlier with my brother. He, too, had been a born-again college student, and on that trip there *had* been a debate. At one point my brother summed up his argument thus, were we to crash and die that instant, he would go to heaven and I to hell. Though I laughed at the sophomoric certainty with which he stated this, the thought was to take hold, would surface at times such as this cold Iowa night. I was concerned not with the truth or falseness of the tenet but with its effect. My mother was born-again, having traded the passivity of a Lutheran for the zeal of a Baptist. And though I dismissed as post-adolescent exuberance my brother's evangelism, I could not do so with hers. She had brought to her faith a heartfelt conviction, would no doubt die with this conviction (and this I envied), and now worried as only a mother can over the fate of my soul. I was powerless to comfort her, except by mouthing certain precepts and living certain lies, and this I would never do.

My mother was a northern woman in a southern land. And, though the South is reputedly a bastion of religious fervor, my mother—in the country town of Enola—found herself alone with her zeal. Not that religion was the only difference. Letters and phone calls over the years had imparted to me the uniqueness of her situation. The weather of course was different, warmer, in its own way as siege-like as the coldness of the North; and the light was different, the vegetation more desperate and grisly, the poverty of the rural areas more apparent in the listing barns and fallow fields. Arkansas lacked the Scandinavian neatness of Minnesota, the precise order of seasons. Doctors walked into examining rooms smoking cigarettes, eight-year-olds chewed tobacco, cars were blocked on front yards.

Though my mother was too much of a lady to ever say so, I suspect she suspected a mental weakness on the part of most southerners, their polite but maddening slowness, their taoistic manner of taking all blame unscathed, their Oriental humility. I thought I understood my mother's alienation, and it had little to do with the average Southerner's intelligence. I once spent six months in Baltimore, and, though I made friends and have pleasant memories, I could never pass through a thin alienation, an awareness of not quite belonging to the dark-haired, short- statured crowd around me. So too, my mother, despite the presence of genuine southern hospitality (and no place is more earnestly friendly than the South), could never quite fit in, never see that southern light as did the natives.

My mother sustained her religion via long distance, watching Billy Graham on television, listening to gospel radio shows, sending for tracts. She introduced me to God in a way I'll never forget. When I was five or six I experienced one of those catastrophic funks only children are capable of, and, walking by our dog, a brown-and-black beagle named Corky, who lifted his head and wagged his tail at my approach, I kicked him fully in the mouth. My mother saw this and made me sit in a corner as punishment. The real punishment, however, came before the corner, when my mother said, "What do you think God thinks of boys who kick their dogs?" And right there God was created, and guilt nudged its way permanently into my psyche. All this in a way I don't completely understand. Up till then I had strode the world guiltlessly. It had never occurred to me God would be watching, shaking his hoary head.

But if religion fostered guilt, it also absolved it. When my brother was a toddler he had fallen down the basement steps of our farmhouse one day. There came a loud serial bumping, an ear-splitting squeal, then silence. My parents rushed down the basement midst a flurry of questions. "Who left the door open?" "Is he breathing?" "What's the doctor's number?" I had left that door open. I slipped outside and ran behind the granary, hiding between it and an ocean wave of a snowdrift, kneeling in the snow, clasping my hands the way my mother had taught me, praying for my brother to live, praying to hoary, head-shaking God.

My mother did not come by her conversion till I was an adult, and my religious upbringing had been but weekly doses of staid Lutheranism. Church was not some vaulted, apse-filled cathedral but a steepled crackerbox; not monks huddled in antechambers but Ernest the hardware-store owner passing the collection plate; not holy water in silver chalices but black coffee in Styrofoam cups.

But to encounter religion in the South was to explore vistas of unpretentiousness. On my last visit to my parents I had borrowed their station wagon and spent an afternoon exploring the area, the two-lane roads, the listing barns and fallow fields, the crossroads towns of Barney and Skunk Hollow and Ambrose. At one point I came upon a white-clapboard church set back from the road. I stopped the station wagon and backed up and wished for a camera. There, standing by the shoulder at the end of a dirt driveway, large as life, was a plywood cutout of Jesus. It was a typically Western Jesus, with long brown hair and blue eyes, everything outlined in black like a cartoon. Indeed, a cartoon-like balloon swelled from Jesus' mouth, the words written in a more or less Gothic script: "All are welcome."

What prosaic mysticism was this? The fate of one's soul intermediated by a sheet of plywood? I never recall this image without another surfacing. Its origin I know not. Perhaps it is an old dream, or one I am yet to have. There stands a church on a hill, and outside the church stands a man. He is dressed in work clothes, sleeves rolled up, head bowed, and he is listening to the pastor inside sing an old country hymn, and around the man and the church is the land, the hills and hollows and flats, the woods thick and concealing, gnarled oaks from which niggers were lynched, where men inbred with daughters and traded wives for goats, where teeth rotted and dogs were cursed, where all manner of atrocities were committed with grinning pleasure, if sin exists it is this, and the man is outside the clapboard church, hearing the song, the call, the gnarled oaks, "You must become as a child," fists clenched, head bowed, misery and anguish rising from his loins on up, save him dear God, save him from this horror and beauty and glistening mundanity, he is half-erect, half-bowed, his spirit yearning, his body dragging, come take him, Jesus, come take him home...

I no longer "understood" religion, could in good faith neither embrace nor mock it. I had no answer for the black night outside the car windows, nor the blackness waiting for my crash. What was my shield? Having approached my literary struggles with a cavalier attitude, deeming it better to fail and know then never know at all, I now questioned the wisdom of this philosophy. Was it worthwhile to struggle day after day at such a frustrating task, hewing and forcing and wedging words that would most likely be laughed at, if indeed read at all? Would the acid of cynicism ever be stayed?

# 3.

The kid dropped me off twenty miles south of Des Moines. It was near midnight and traffic was sparse, solitary pairs of headlights bearing down from the north, gusting by in a flurry of dry grit. Long cold minutes separated the rush of headlights, and, after standing half an hour or so under the interchange lights, giving what traffic passed a chance to see me, I shouldered my pack and walked south into the darkness. Though paring my already slim chances of catching a ride, such a decision had an instinctual validity, as if motion equaled, if not warmth, then at least life.

I shuffled along the shoulder, a metaphor of the human condition, some bipedal crustacean scuttling the ocean floor of night. I was committed to this trip by both time and distance, and could ill afford the weakening effects of doubt. I decided to walk a little farther, try a few more vehicles, then find a windbreak and wait the night in my sleeping bag.

The bag carried a certain amount of history. Robert had lent it to me on our last trip together, yet another cathartic motorcycle journey through the Southwest. Robert, unlike myself, was a real traveler. Hailing from Williston, North Dakota, inheritor of more land and sky than one man dare claim, Robert had chosen again and again the road, spurning employment at and subsequent ownership of his father's bakery. Robert had spent three years on a shoestring tour of the world—Europe, India, Africa, Australia—and on his return to Williston (hitching a ride at sunset in a '48 Plymouth) found his father dead and the bakery sold. He gravitated towards the Twin Cities and eventually settled down there in the early Seventies. Or if not settled down, then at least set up a base from which to launch his innumerable trips. Robert was forever planning great fanciful expeditions, motorcycle trips to Alaska, safaris across the Australian outback, treasure hunting in the Bahamas. Never easy to pull off—Robert would work a double-shift for months to finance them—these trips became fewer and fewer over the years, with fewer and fewer people joining him.

I had joined him, for a while, on his last trip. I will always remember Robert astride his black Triumph motorcycle, clad in his bombardier's jacket, an oversized leather wallet chained to his belt, clumsy hiking boots, long blond hair and wire-rimmed glasses left over from the late Sixties, eyes that had seen *it*. We spent most of that winter in Texas, working daily labor jobs in San Antonio (where I experienced the most debilitating hangover of my life). In northwestern Texas we climbed the highest point in the state, Guadalupe Peak, 8351 feet above sea level. We shared a can of cold green beans at the top, the desert spreading hundreds of miles around us, the wind constant and sharp, the sun descending into haze. Robert and I talked about travelling. It was a strange discussion, and I remember it chiefly for its immediacy. We'd had the discussion many times, actually, in bars and tents and coffee shops, a reiteration of our belief in the road, our antipathy towards things established, our assertions of never settling down. But a strain of desperateness haunted the dialogue this time, an urgency in the tone of our platitudes and vigorousness of our assents, an urgency that did not carry far in the desert twilight.

We split up at a McDonald's in Phoenix. Robert had six dollars and intentions of selling blood. I continued out to

California, then up the coast to Washington and eventually east to Minnesota, determined to write.

Why did we take such trips? What did they prove? The road had always tempted me, or if not the road then some wild freedom it later came to represent. A great number of my childhood daydreams centered on running away from home, not to the circus or a large city but to the woods or mountains or jungle, to a place of delicious privacy. Why I so desired this privacy is hard to say. I wasn't mistreated; I certainly had enough time alone. It may be that I was actually yearning for responsibility for my own life. To travel is to accept responsibility.

Only once had I seriously attempted to run away. My family lived a few months in San Diego, joining thousands of others in that mid-Sixties migration to the Golden Coast. One night I sneaked out of our rented house, my pillowcase serving as backpack, and stood at the end of our driveway. The house stood on Brandywine Hill, and I beheld San Diego as never before, a neon megacity, a constellation of uncaring lights, oblivious to the dreams of a schoolboy. I stood as though on an Acapulcan cliff, equally loathe to dive or turn back. But turn back I did, sliding open the patio door and slinking to the room I shared with my brother. I fell asleep to my father's snoring.

Were my later trips but reenactments of this thwarted escape? Had I traded the forest and mountains and jungles for the road, the only real wilderness left for me, that indeed ever existed? What was I rushing to meet?

The odd moments I pondered motivation for my literary quest, I thought back to the conversation on Guadalupe Peak. By writing I could simultaneously "make something of myself" (a previously dormant aspect of my make-up having arisen in my mid-twenties) while eschewing the conventional lifestyle I found so abhorrent. That my plan had not yet reached fruition—I was as far from making something of

myself as could be, and the only thing glaringly
unconventional about my lifestyle was its indigence — gave
me small concern. Like the situation I was now in, scratching
barely discernible progress through the midst of night, I at
least knew in what direction I was heading.

A car stopped, coming to rest at a forty-five degree angle
to the shoulder. The driver was a Chicano with a
pockmarked face, and I could tell at a glance he was drunk.
He sat slouched in his seat, staring at me with a thin smile, as
though recalling some secret we had shared since childhood.
With abandon now frightening, I climbed into the car. At the
very least I would die warm.

His name was Vic, and on his invitation I began helping
myself to a cooler of Budweisers in the back seat. Vic was on
his way to Austin, Texas, and he was travelling in comfort.
Janis Joplin's *Pearl* album was reeling through an eight-track
under the dash. A packet of white crosses and a bag of
weed — again proffered and again accepted — were cached
above the sun visors. Apparently the only laws Vic observed
were those of physics, and these but grudgingly. Sometimes
reaching one hundred miles an hour (I could not help but
"nonchalantly" glance at the speedometer), he would swoop
behind other vehicles, passing on the right or left at the last
second, tires squealing like suckling pigs, my right leg flexing
an imaginary brake. Not infrequently Vic would yell "Piss
stop!" and lock up the wheels, coming to a stop more or less
on the shoulder. I joined him on the second piss stop, arcing
my stream into the ditch while staring straight up, stars
undiffused by city light, wind blowing from the north, the car
panting beside us. I liked Vic, and I liked what he represented,
an anarchic freedom I would never completely embrace, an
ability to get stone drunk, drive one hundred miles an hour,
turn an interstate into a urinal trough.

I once worked with a man who had hitched a ride with Neal Cassady. Or at least I choose to believe he had. Several of us had been playing poker at lunch, and the conversation had turned to hitchhiking stories. Ray, an iron-haired, leather-faced grinder, told of being picked up by a man who drove one hundred miles an hour the entire length of Ohio, Ray's arm cemented to the dash. I asked when this had happened. He wasn't sure, either the late Forties or early Fifties. Had the guy talked much? "Talked?" said Ray. "He talked my goddamn ears off!"

Later that week I brought in Ann Charter's biography of Kerouac and showed Ray pictures of Neal Cassady, asking if that had been the man. But it had happened over two decades ago, and Ray, despite holding the book at arm's length and scratching his grey crewcut, could not remember.

I suppose there have been many Cassadys. One of my earliest heroes was my cousin Joel. A dozen years my senior, Joel taught me how to comb my hair like Elvis, talked knowingly of sex, drove hotrod Plymouths full blast; he could fine-tune V-8 engines, poke girls in back seats, roll packs of Camels in his sleeves...

...gone now, faded, like dust settling on a dirt road after a car has passed...

Vic and I ran out of beer around Kansas City. We stopped at a 7-11 only to find the precious fluid locked behind coolers. We could not but stare at the cans of Miller and Pabst and Budweiser, lunulars of condensation on the glass doors, thick chains draped through the handles. The clerk eyed us warily, no doubt having experienced raucous protest at such a state of affairs. But neither Vic nor I expressed other than mild annoyance. We were simply too late.

We spent the last part of the night in a motel off the Will Rogers Turnpike, ingesting a queasy breakfast the next morning in the motel's coffee shop. Vic spent a good deal of time rubbing his forehead and the back of his neck, his

Cassadean fervor apparently dissipated. He drove almost normally this Sunday morning. We shook hands on a bridge spanning Interstate 40, Vic predicting we would meet again.

I hopped over guard rails and waded through brown grass, making my way to I-4O, changing direction from south to east. The day was so fresh and brisk and sunny that for a long time I just walked along the shoulder, not even bothering to thumb for a ride.

# 4.

Travelling like this within a structured framework of time, an abstention of home life rather than abandonment, had its own peculiar freedom. Though in the background loomed the spectre of a real trip (and what has one to prove?), I enjoyed right now this short-lived exuberance, this onrush of people and scenery and weather.

I'd stuck to the interstates out of practicality, though I was not unaware of a certain irony in my choice. As with television and the I.R.S., I had once detested the streamlined highways with their eternal sameness, the numerical pretensions of mile markers, the constant wind. But gradually I had come to appreciate the interstates for what they were: the ultimate road, where, in theory at least, one never has to stop, can cruise endlessly, can realize the American dream. This was the road my father was searching for.

The interstates were made for my father and those like him, men driving cars with V-8 engines and hydraflow transmissions and panoramic windshields. They paid for gas out of their pockets, trusted their car to the man with the star, took two weeks off every summer.

I had been thinking of my father a lot this morning. Perhaps it was because of the Oklahoma landscape, the brown stiff grass and random clumps of poplars and cottonwood, the long rises and descensions, the miniature buttes and mesas. Though hailing from greener, more rolling country, he had spent time in and traversing through the Dustbowl of the Thirties, riding the rails to his half-sister's house in Los Angeles, hitchhiking back via tired jalopies, eventually joining what was to be the last of the Horse Cavalry. For me this was knowledge of a stranger, did not jibe with the man who left the verdant lawns of suburbia everyday for work.

As a child—before my family's move to suburbia—I occasionally paged through old scrapbooks kept in the attic of our farmhouse, sitting cross-legged on the plank floor, leaning against the claw-footed Victrola. (The attic was an eerie place, and I only dared enter it during daylight. At night I would stare at my bedroom ceiling, aware of the slightest creaking, the softest thud, emanating from above. In truth, the attic was inhabited, by bats, and my father and Uncle Chet spent a macabre Saturday afternoon vacuuming sleeping, upside-down bats into my mother's Eureka, then removing the squeaking, heavy-clothed bag and submerging it in a water trough.) The scrapbooks were filled with yellowed newspaper clippings, headlines of World War Two, ration books, black-and white Kodak prints, telegrams between my parents, their romance played out against the backdrop of a global war. I found it unsettling to see my parents so young, my mother with long hair and bangs, my father with dark curls and a thin neck. Here he was with several shipmates in the navy. They were squatting on the ground and holding a pelican, wings outstretched, a makeshift cardboard sign before the hapless bird, "USS Lapon." Here he was with my mother in a wooden booth in a New York restaurant, sitting side by side, a beer bottle in my father's hand, my mother wearing a pillbox hat. My father changed most. To follow the clippings and photographs chronologically, to turn from one scrapbook to the next, was to see a man not only age—gain weight, lose hair, acquire glasses—but to actually, inwardly, change. In the early pictures my father was always smiling, in later ones frowning. I would earnestly study those edge-curled photographs, as though to discern with a child's intuition what had happened.

For something had indeed happened. With the passing of years I found my father wanted nothing more than to supplant my dreams with his. He was a particularly avid sports fan, often placing one television atop another and watching two games simultaneously. But this passion had refused genetic transmission. The formative years of my childhood had been spent on our dying farm, where I wandered fields with my dog, explored abandoned houses, hurled cattail spears at prehistoric monsters. Upon our move to the suburbs—a move coinciding with my entry into that most hideous of environments, that of junior high school—I discovered I was not only expected to participate in team sports but to do so gleefully, as if the greatest thing on earth was to grovel in the dirt with other boys. My father held the belief that any boy should want more than anything to "play ball," and expected me to personify this axiom. The coaches, for the most part, were stupid shallow men, concerned not with instilling life principles or lessons in morality but only with winning and losing. Inhabiting a reed-thin, hollow-chested body, my eyes circled by rings of dark-blue, I preferred books to cross-body blocks. As with all children, I was forever trying to balance the demands of the world against its realities. My father had virtually ordered me to join football, and I had neither the guts nor the heart to tell him I had failed.

Having failed to make the Johanna Junior High football team, and this in a scholastic sports structure that, like the army, accepted everyone, I proceeded to construct the greatest hoax of my life. I spent afternoons not on the gridiron but in the school library, riding the activity bus home with Spanish club students and real football players. Upon confronting my father and his inevitable questions—how many tackles I'd made, how many passes caught, touchdowns scored—I came up with fiction bordering on Chekovian realism, portraying myself as a competent, though certainly not outstanding, tight end. My father worked nights and was not able to attend any of my "games," thus saving me from ultimate disclosure.

A white Buick pulled over. The driver was a middle-aged man, with grey hair combed back from a widow's peak. He was solicitous of my comfort, suggesting I remove my coat so as to feel warmer when returning outside, explaining how my seat reclined, offering cigarettes.

The boundaries of Oklahoma City fell behind us. Then came "something to read," a book "left by another hitchhiker" that he pulled from under his seat. I paged through it. The book was an oversized paperback, black-and-white photographs of husky young men named Bob and Bill and Max, a paragraph under each photo relating the "plot." I staved a rising paranoia. What if the guy pulled a gun and drove off into the bushes, there to saw-DO-mize me? A minute or two of road silence crept by. I asked him if he had a family.

I knew it was an asinine question. I knew the guy could be the personification of manhood, have sired eighteen children and laid half the women in Oklahoma City, and still be queer as a three-dollar bill. At least I knew this intellectually. That I asked meant prejudice was lying beneath my liberal veneer, rearing at the slightest hint of danger.

The man nodded his head. Sure, he had a family, a brother back in the city, a sister on a ranch thirty miles north. I waited vainly for him to speak of wife and kids (especially kids, oh Matthews!). I told him to let me off at the next exit.

I watched the Buick recede under the noonday sun, and fear gave way to sympathy. Interstate love. I'm on a tall building. What if I had accepted the man's pathetic highway seduction? What if I jump? There is alienation everywhere, these Oklahoma hills where no one belongs.

# 5.

I was intensely aware of being in Oklahoma. This was Dust Bowl country. My father had ridden a freight train across this land. I tried to imagine it through his eyes, my father leaning against the door of an empty cattle car, legs braced against the sway of the rail, staring out at dust and wind and abandoned farms. All day secondhand memories had been rising, an odd commingling of printed words and celluloid images. I thought of Steinbeck's Joad family, of Henry Fonda as Tom Joad, and Jane Darwell as his mother, spending her last few minutes in the old farmhouse, the jalopy outside packed and ready to go, Ma Joad alone in the square empty house, sorting through the scant memorabilia of her life, a postcard from the New York World's Fair, a thimble-sized ceramic Scottish terrier, the dog seeming almost alive in the hazy close-up of the film, tears in the darkness of the theatre, and tears for the end.

Where will you go, Tom? Where will you stay? Wherever there's a cop beating up a guy, Ma, I'll be there. Wherever some company's trying to bust a union, I'll be there. I'll be in the look of kids' eyes when they ain't got enough for supper...

An irrepressible sadness haunted these hills and plains and dwarf buttes. The Okies had traveled out of necessity, desperation, and to do so is to enter a bleak existence. I have seen old drifters. But did not every man have an exodus, whether inner or external? Was not every man, in some ways, an Okie from the Thirties? Did not man flee from tragedy to greater tragedy?

My father had fled, once by rail and later by bottle. I had tried to flee as a youngster, and on later trips, with the naked freedom of a motorcycle. I had "come of age" in the late Sixties, and my father and I adhered to the polarity of the times like magnetized filings. Any topic—hair length, Viet Nam, the draft—could set off horrendous arguments, both of us debating more with our lungs than our brains. Leaving on my first road trip, my first abandonment of job and family and friends, fully eighteen years old, I stopped at the factory where my father worked. He was a foreman and had his own office of sorts, coils of electrical wire looped on the pegboard walls, stacks of partially disassembled motors, the inevitable pinups. I stood before his desk, clad in riding leathers, helmet in hand. My father's life had been a struggle, an uphill climb from country to city to suburb, and I was expected to go— where? Out to yet farther suburbs? To not only turn my back on this quest, but to despise it, seemed my only choice. We said goodbye awkwardly. My father and I did not hug. We never hugged. We shook hands.

A man in a Ford Econoline van was my next benefactor. He was a few years older than me, talkative, friendly. Yep, those were his two sons in the back. He was divorced and only got to see 'em every other weekend. Had to take 'em back to the old lady up in Tulsa. Yeah, he worked back in the city, drove a cement truck, heavy equipment and all that. Lived here all his life. Anything I wanted to know about Oklahoma, just ask.

We talked about the Depression and the dust bowl days, or more accurately he talked and I listened (a hitchhiking trip is really one long conversation). The man asked if I liked Woody Guthrie. I said he was a hero of mine. Well, now, if the guy was, like I said, an idol, well, if I wanted we could swing off and see the house Woody had been born in. Wouldn't take long.

We pulled off at Okemah. Woody's house was outside of town, not so much hidden as overcome by a patch of cottonwood. Not much was there, a large square hole filled with rotting lumber. I felt equally indignant and satisfied. What kind of memorial was this? But then what did I want, another Graceland?

The framework of one wall still stood, supporting a section of lath and plaster shaped like the state of Maine. Graffiti covered Maine, and I noticed my name. I was in love with Becky.

# 6.

Two women in a Camaro picked me up at twilight. They were circumferentially travelling the United States, now on a southern leg home to New York. They looked east coast—dark-haired, small-framed, probodiscean—and, after learning I had no marijuana, suggested I buy a six-pack of beer at the next stop. I assented. My passage thus paid, I rode ignored half the length of Arkansas.

The sun set fast behind us, the land becoming hilly and forested, swamped with early shadow. I entered into lone contemplation. I became nervous about my arrival. How much had my parents aged this time? They seemed to age in cycles, at times appearing much as I had last seen them, at others shockingly older. We played against each other, mutual barometers of mortality. Would they, as I noticed their greying hair, their stooped postures, their occasional absent-mindedness, notice the emergence of my own wrinkles, the receding of my own hair, the burden of my own troubles?

And what about my father? Occasionally, I like to think that in another era, a more historically placid epoch, we would have gotten along famously, though under honest scrutiny I had to deny this. Something in our arguments transcended politics and culture. And though in recent years we had reached an accord, a kind of sullen compromise, I knew its core was hollow, a reconciliation aided more by distance and separation than any convergence of beliefs.

On my last visit I'd had an argument with my father, an upheaval from days of old. Though initially political, something about the moral validity of capital punishment, it had quickly turned personal, and I was surprised at the power of emotions long dormant. Later that evening, sitting with my parents in the living room, watching television, I covertly studied my father—much like my childhood rearview mirror scrutiny—and I could not deny that, were I to see him as a stranger, he would be but an old man. The evidence was there, the grey wispy hair, the flesh wrinkled and spotted with age, the chin dissolving into jowls. Something reached out in me, and I was enveloped in the pathos of childhood. To a child a father is life itself and death is as far away as the end of summer vacation. I said goodbye to a child's mortality that night. Tears came to my eyes. I rose from the sofa, for I was quite powerless to stop those tears, and stepped out into the back yard.

Huge, moth-like snowflakes were falling. I made my way to the back of the barn, leaning against it, looking out over fields half-covered with snow. A dog howled from far away. It is a dog's night, I thought, this deep thick night of the South, in which I stand a stranger and yet am part of, its blood my blood, for the North has nothing for me really, no impellation so deep as to make the lost and wayward soul cry out, vow to return and never leave, and I stand in the half-frozen loam, crying not because I would soon lose my father but because I lost him long ago, and I wonder where he went, where all fathers went, big men driving big cars surely through the night, with work-hardened forearms and assurances that everything is all right, perfectly all right, and it was, my confidence in fathers was supreme, eagerly accepted, never doubted, men who would cross their legs and I would crawl through the porthole of a submarine and emerge upon a father's lap, listening while he talked with other men, other fathers, and he saw in me the future and I my future in him, our eyes meeting with the most comfortable seeing I have ever felt, my father could lift up a car, beat up any number of bad guys, dispel bedroom terrors. And his tools! Those mysterious tools, the pipewrench and pliers and soldering gun, hung and scattered in the basement workshop, I would sneak down and play with them, heft their weight, guess their function, these tools had been forged before I was born, waiting along with my father as I passed through the ether of pre-life. So what went wrong? Did I destroy this friendship, or did he, or did we both? And something happens and a father cannot remain a father, becomes just another older man demanding things of me I could never in my constitution deliver. Don't go away, Dad, don't walk down that ill-defined, barely perceived road. I know you're waiting and want with all your heart for me to join you but I can't! I love you from between my cells and you are the one man on earth who can still make me cry and this is the message I will never send, even though when you are gone, really gone, I will wish I had sent something, did something, said something, like the time we sat together in the front pew of Calvary Baptist Church, your own father lying in a casket before the altar, and I knew you wished you could bring him back, tell him things you could never tell him, but it was late, very late, and man moves through this sad and funny life not knowing the heartaches and mistakes waiting. Oh Dad! Don't let it be too late. Come back from that road. Or at least don't look at me going down my own road, forever and ever down my own road.

# BOOK THREE

# THE FINDING OF A THEME

# 1.

I wrote more than ever that winter, the *Omni* rejection staying my enthusiasm but temporarily. Indeed, after a rueful and renovative introspection, a week spent shoring up my confidence with rationalizations now forgotten, I emerged more determined than ever, eager to tip my Underwood at the windmills of publishing.

But along with this rekindled enthusiasm came a certain maturing, a realization—like a miner's lamp glowing in the dust of a cave-in—that there were aspects of my craft I could improve. Abandoning the newspaper-magazine approach to learning grammar, I finally walked to the branch library on Eighteenth and checked out a book on the subject. On the same shelf were several books dealing with the less mechanistic side of composition, the creative-writing tomes. I instinctively mistrusted these books, fearing that formulaic instruction would destroy whatever was beginning to creep out, as if the greater my independence the more pure my "art." And yet in many ways I felt so lost, so unsure if I had made anything resembling progress, that I could not resist their allure. Quelling a feeling of self-betrayal, I checked out the *1979 Writer's Handbook*, one hundred chapters by writers about writing, reasoning that such a cross-section would distill any corrosion of independence.

I spent that weekend reading the book. It was much like mine and Robert's barroom literary conversations: fascinating, dangerous, inherently forbidden. Lying on my bed, a cup of coffee in various stages of tepidness on the floor beside me, an ashtray balanced on my stomach, I read of the various do's and don'ts, the intrinsic mores, of creative writing. Specificity was stressed repeatedly by the authors, as was the need to show rather than tell. These and other suggestions made good sense. Some advice was more open to question. One author reported success, publication-wise, after discovering a "threefold" technique, three being the magic number when it came to plot, phrasing, adjectives. Others, assuming the neophyte writer had no aspirations to greatness, instructed how to obtain the next best thing — prolificness. (Just what I wanted, thousands of pages of mediocre writing.) The impression I received that weekend, reading between the lines and the lines themselves, was that composition was a befuddling, mysterious affair, too alive to contain within rules and suggestions, and most successfully approached with the wisdom of hindsight. Closing the book late that Sunday night, all the advice and suggestions and hints absorbed into my consciousness, I felt I had received, more than anything, pats on the back, formulaic encouragement to a fellow traveler.

But, if not keys to prosaic mystery, there were at least forms of solace in those pages. I took heart, particularly, from advice not to worry about imitating other writers, one's voice having out despite oneself. I aped whomever I happened to be reading — Kerouac, Steinbeck, Thomas Wolfe. The latter in particular had a powerful effect on my writing. One chapter of *The Web and the Rock* spawned days of Wolfean paragraphs, clause piled upon clause, no detail too small to omit, no event too ordinary to remain unexalted. These were plotless, aimless, mindless attempts, inevitably bogging down in a morass of adjectives, beyond which shined no beacon, no signal, towards which to struggle.

The trip to my parents, combined with the *Omni* rejection, signified what I perceived as a new direction in my writing (I wanted things to happen fast). Returning to my cold and stale apartment (Mrs. McAdams had shut off the heat in my absence), I vowed to take stock not only of my writing but of myself, to dig into the trenches of winter. I spent hours compartmentalizing my papers, sorting them into folders labeled "Manuscripts Submitted," "Manuscripts Unfinished," "Possible Stories." I cleaned and oiled the Underwood, washed seasons-old laundry, pared my fingernails.

Other aspects of my life bore inspection. With Minneapolis under siege of winter, I was fast becoming a city hermit. Possessing neither phone nor television, scarcely glancing at headlines as I leafed through the occasional newspaper to reach the comics, I lived life insulated from those global events deemed important by society. Robert stopped by once a week or so, providing news of the "outside" world, much like some latter-day Marco Polo bearing tales of a strange and distant land. I first heard of the hostages in Iran through him, Robert claiming I was the last person in America to have known.

But in many ways, important ways, I did not feel isolated at all. The world I was shutting out was a world I did not believe in. I did not believe Tide got laundry 40% cleaner, or that Ivory was 99 & 44/100% pure, or that Winston tasted like a cigarette should. I didn't believe in voting for one jerk over another, or that Communism was threatening to engulf the world, or that watching the evening news could be considered anything but entertainment. I did not believe in doing ten things I hated doing everyday, in any kind of mindless work ethic, that Dale Carnegie had anything to be optimistic about.

But I did admit to some sociologic perception. I was all too aware, with the numeralogical superstition inherent in any member of a society thriving on the concept of time, that I now resided in the year 1980. One. Nine. Eight. Zero. The numbers themselves were austere, forbidding. While never having marched in protest or burned draft cards in front of recruiting stations, I had still ridden the coattails of the hippie dream, had toked the hashpipe and grown my hair. I believed it inevitable society would change. But the dream had been extinguished, or more accurately assimilated, by the time 1980 arrived, a year that came too soon, and yet couldn't have come fast enough.

The sub-zero temperatures proved too much for my truck, and I was forced to use the bus system for getting to work. Though waiting for a Minneapolis bus in January is not time spent in heaven, there was much about riding the red lumbering beasts that I liked. Boarding the number Ten every afternoon at Central and Twentieth, I would sit as far back in the bus as possible, there to mentally describe the "convex ears," "fisheyed profiles," "voluminous ankles" of my fellow passengers. Disembarking in downtown Minneapolis, I would wait an indeterminate amount of time on the corner of Fourth and Washington for a number Seven. The city was in the midst of a frantic rejuvenation that winter, brick and gabled buildings being replaced seemingly overnight by glass and chrome geometric statements. A bone-white monolith was under construction directly across the street, and, as I huddled in my greatcoat, the January wind blowing dry snow and grit and the diesel smell of downtown, I would daily mark progress of the building. At first I despised the structure, viewing it as an example of mindless corporatism, but later came to identify with its construction, to feel empathy with the ant-like workers, as if the building were a symbol of my own goals.

Near the end of January came four or five days where I drank too much, sitting night after night on a stool at Momart's, hoisting seven-ounce glasses of Schmidt mouthwards till a great watery bloat overcame me. I would then negotiate the uneven and ice-encrusted sidewalks back to my room, there to stare at the Underwood several seconds before plopping in bed, spending the remainder of the night in a state not dissimilar to sleep. Two nights running I became ill, possessing on the second night not even the strength to crawl to the toilet. During those rare moments I sought motivation for such behavior, I liked to think I was seeking relief from my titanic literary struggles. But deep down I realized the absurdity of such an answer. I drank simply out of loneliness, loneliness that had been graphically exposed on a city bus.

Riding home one night down Minnehaha Avenue, I noticed a pretty, sandy-haired woman climb aboard. I fell in love. The way she dug in her large purse for fare, balancing against the acceleration of the bus as she dropped change in the counter, then scanning the interior for a seat, all had such an air of tragic, graceful vulnerability — reminding me of Greta Garbo in Grand Hotel — that I could be not but awestruck. Incredibly, she sat in the seat before me.

Having let my share of "opportunities" slip past in life, I was occasionally able to screw up enough courage to make the first move. And the best way was to plunge, don't think, hesitate, reflect, just do it! The bus rolled along like time itself. To speak or not to speak. I had been with certain men when a woman passed by, in bars and workplaces, and had been embarrassed by their catcalls, their whistles and boorish invitations. But on a certain level I envied their nerve (not to mean tons of nerve; had any of the women called these men on their harassment, and a few did, the men would be, and were, rendered dumbstruck), such behavior at least possessing life compared to my own gravelike actions. A middle ground had to exist, an area I occasionally stumbled into.

"Does this bus go downtown?" I blurted.

The sandy-haired woman turned halfway round, profiling a slightly upturned nose. "I think so, but I never ride it that far. I get off at St. Mary's."

"Are you a nurse or something?"

"No. I go there for O.T." She faced me. "Do you know what that is?"

I guessed "occupational therapy." She nodded, seemed about to say something, then looked out the window. There, swathed in asphalt blackness, was St. Mary's Hospital. She quickly pulled the bell rope and walked to the front, stutter-stepping as the bus dove to a stop. The woman turned to me, smiled, mouthed the word "bye," then stepped off.

Though an ordinary enough encounter, its memory clung tenaciously, inhabiting my thoughts at odd times: as I swept the warehouse at work, drew a bath, worked a new ribbon into the Underwood — giving rise to all manner of fantasy. Who was the woman? Why was she taking therapy? She had walked away from the bus with an apparently normal gait, thus reinforcing the more romantic notion of her problem being psychological. I believed her above all to be a survivor of tragedy.

I rode the same bus at the same time for weeks afterwards, but the sandy-haired woman never reappeared. I began to think something had happened to her, that some turn of events had swept her irretrievably away. The night I gave up was very cold. As usual I had ridden into downtown, disembarking on Eighth and walking to Marquette, there to wait for the Central Avenue bus. The corner I stood on faced north, the entire block having recently been razed. Now, the sterile light of a full moon shining on the rubble and payloaders and snowdrifts before me, the wind howling loneliness as it found sudden freedom, the Minneapolis skyline looming phosphorescent and impossibly large, a feeling of desolate ownership came over me, a sovereignty brought on by solitude within and without.

I heard a scraping of boots. A parka-hooded figure approached and stood a few feet distant. It was a middle-aged Asian man, waiting, like me, for the bus. Not one word passed between us. I found it comforting to stand in silence with this man, this sub-zero crystalline night, resting, actually, in a place language did not belong.

# 2.

Ralph and Alice stopped over one night with "important" news. Ralph was wearing a dark-blue suit with sleeves that were too short, a trace of camphor about the garment. Alice — portently swollen Alice — stood next to him, her arm laced through his, and, though she was actually taller than Ralph, seemed somehow to look up at him, to psychically raise him five inches off the floor.

With the expression of a child about to disclose what will surely bring praise, a report card of A's or some such nonsense, Ralph informed me I was now living beneath the best encyclopedia salesman in northeast Minneapolis. Yep, he was going after the big money, none of this minimum-wage crap for him. Apparently having answered some Amway-like ad, those that troll for people "unafraid" of success, of big homes and new cars and gargantuan bank accounts, Ralph was now fully, thoroughly, sappily indoctrinated. He had bought a tie, shined his shoes, and was to spend next week being trained in. Ralph expounded at length about the grand future that lay waiting, awkwardly using sentence structures he must have already been memorizing. He would receive a commission of ten percent, which was a pretty darn good commission for any salesman, much less one just starting out. A set of encyclopedias sold for 1200 dollars, therefore each sale garnered 120 bucks, just like that! And they sold like the proverbial hotcakes. And they could tell just by looking at Ralph he'd be a terrific salesman. That the company provided no base salary, no benefits, no insurance, mattered not at all. With the kind of money Ralph was going to make who had to worry about stuff like that?

Before leaving, Ralph insinuated I might care to get in on this bonanza, glancing (or did I just imagine it?) at the Underwood. I begged off, allowing that I wasn't the "type." And in truth I wasn't. I'd always considered myself too clever, too morally developed, to fall for get-rich-quick schemes. Actually, I was simply bored by such matters. Nothing put me to sleep faster than talk of municipal bonds or the Dow Jones average. I equated money, or at least the pursuit of money, with settling down, with conforming, with not only submitting to but helping forge and initial a very personal set of leg irons. When I thought of money beyond the concept of take-home pay, it was as something I would acquire grandiosely, inadvertently, through writing or being discovered by Hollywood or winning a lottery. Until then, I was content.

Every morning a rust-eaten Buick pulled up and honked, and Ralph, like some mesomorphic Dagwood Bumstead, would dash down the steps and out the door, black briefcase in hand, squeezing into the car with several other suited young men. I would mentally wish him luck, then turn to my writing. Parallels came unbidden. Was I, in my own way, donning a suit and tie every morning and springing down that sidewalk to success? Ralph spread shoe leather, I spread ink. How much was my commission?

As if the old version weren't powerful enough, my psyche came up with a new strain of guilt. Though writing prodigiously, I suffered from a lack of focus, starting dozens of stories, poems, essays, novels, and abandoning all with equal diffidence. I realized the need of having a plan, an outline, a goal, but I could land on nothing inspiring enough, or, more to the point, could not sustain inspiration. Once I lost interest (usually within the top third of the page), had a gun, that erstwhile symbol of the utmost in motivation, been pointed at my head, I could have typed not one satisfactory word more.

Thus my first encounter with writer's block, a condition that, having never experienced it, I had cretinously concluded was not in my lot. I thought of Pirsig, writing in *Zen and the Art of Motorcycle Maintenance* of the stripped screw, the impossible-to-remove bolt, the first wall. But I couldn't remember his advice, if indeed there had been any. I began to question my dedication. I was writing, but I was not writing. I did not pace the floor all night, my brain boiling with unwritten prose. I was not filling orange crates with manuscript. I was not starving, shaking with ague, spending the last of my money on postage for yet one more submission.

And therein lay much of the guilt; in over six months I had submitted but two stories. I'd read of others sending out a new story every two weeks. Realizing I would have to decide on a project and stick with it, inspiration or not, I decided to play my trump card, that which I had feared all along it would boil down to. I would write the definitive biker story.

There was hint of predestination in this choice. Unlike nuclear apocalypse or time travel, I actually knew something about motorcycles, and, though I did not consider myself a "biker" per se, such a lifestyle was not entirely foreign to my own. Both reveled in a slovenly exaltation of life, an insipid contentment created by the gratification of animal desires. I had never worn colors or ridden with anything resembling a gang, but I certainly could extrapolate such experiences. Paging through the biker magazines at Shinder's newsstand, *Easyriders, Supercycle, Iron Horse*, once again comparing cold print against theoretical perfection, I steeped myself in a dangerous and now embarrassing condescension—if I could not get published in a biker magazine, I was not meant to write.

# 3.

Robert left town that February. Having been fired from the sheet-metal factory for consistent tardiness, unable to collect unemployment, tired of living with his aunt, the old nun as he called her, Robert decided a change was necessary. We met at the Mixer's the night before he left, his '61 Mercury packed and gassed and waiting outside.

Several pitchers of Schmidt into the night, Robert confessed he was in love. I was not surprised; Robert had been in love seven or eight times since I had known him. He was strange. Though adhering to an unconventional lifestyle, he was in many aspects Victorian. Robert could drink gallons of beer but eschewed any other drug. Though not religious, he never swore, substituting "darn" and "shucks" for more obscene expletives. And when he fell in love it was at a distance, a chaste arctic flame of passion, directed inevitably at those women least accessible.

Except perhaps this time. Robert was in love with Marcia, a divorcee living in Baltimore. Marcia and her ex-husband Freddie went back to the early Seventies, the Dinkytown days. They had been the first of our circle to marry, and the first to divorce six years later. The divorce had affected me in ways unexpected. I had considered Marcia and Freddie as inseparable as the visages of Mount Rushmore, and such news was like a whisper of mortality. Certain images were ingrained in memory. I would always think of Marcia in bell bottoms, long honey-hued hair parted down the middle, freckles masking her cheeks. In the best sense of the word Marcia had been a hippie, possessing a certain countryness, a rurality in her slightly bowlegged stance, an equine tossing back of her hair that spoke of nature, of earth, of corn-fed innocence. Though having entertained stray thoughts about bedding Marcia (as had doubtless most of the men who had known her), fuzzy-edged montages of twisted sheets and clasped limbs, I never considered such ideas anymore than fantasy. Even after the divorce a certain taboo hung in the air. Maybe it was loyalty to Freddie. Maybe it was a sheet in the wind.

And now Robert was in love with Marcia. Had been even before the divorce, he said. Robert was in a quandary. He was deathly afraid of settling down. Marcia already had one kid. "And that's what scares me," Robert said. "I might be willing to actually live with the rugrat. Am I getting old?"

Pouring our last pitcher of beer, Robert came right out and asked my advice. Should he act or forget? Answering with the confidence of one possessing absolutely no stake in the outcome, I told Robert he should indeed declare his love. He expressed surprise that I would advise him to settle down. "Do it," I said. "That's the only way you'll know for sure."

So Robert left, bound for Baltimore and Marcia's heart. I withdrew yet more into winter, garnering solitude round me like a cloak. I wrote and worked and walked. Though the weather was arctic, the temperature for days never exceeding zero, I forced myself to take walks. To walk in the daytime was to stride two worlds, the snow alive with solar brightness, eye-hurting clarity, dog-pissed snowbanks; and across this ordinary world stretched a shadow world, picket fences with picket shadows, shadows of blue-black vibrating depth, shadows that mocked.

But nights were best. Then I plunged into a universe of solitude, striding the tunneled mazed sidewalks, as if I were really going somewhere, bundled in my greatcoat, boots squeaking, the houses tall and flanking, windows glowing with the cold ember of television, the static exploded plumes of chimneys, the unignorable stars, the numb cheeks, the frosting beard, breath escaping in long white plumes of exhausted thought.

With the sub-zero temperatures, Mrs. McAdams' rooming house became a mansion of drafts. I was forced to huddle my beanbag and typewriter and cement podium around the Dura-flame space heater, its orange and blue flames tonguing the small lattice-work of asbestos. The biker story began taking shape. Sentences wiggled out slower than ever, but with what I viewed as better results. I was becoming fussier, more demanding of my prose, and, while striving for a certain economy, a smoothness in syntax, I also addressed the problem of description. Whereas many neophyte authors (or so I gathered from various accounts) wrote too much description, I penned far too little. The cat killer had strode across miles of featureless landscape; the time traveler had moved about a similarly blank milieu. I now wrote pages of description, idiotic description, irrelevant description, slowing the plot (burdening the plot, description-laden plot, that poor ol' plot) to the pace of a glacier. What inherent interest the story possessed was buried under shovelfuls of imagery.

Though abandoning the project more than once, casting papers across the room like surprised pigeons, yielding to the fleeting allure of less formulated ideas, I always returned, out of guilt, out of responsibility, out of a growing realization that only determination accomplishes anything, that enthusiasm counts for little down the long haul.

Sometimes writing was sheer agony. Never had I felt so mute, so bound within the confines of my skull. I wasted hours over trivialities, centering the paper just right, searching my dictionary for just the right word, getting lost in ramifications having nothing to do with the task at hand. I began writing later and later into the night, kept company by a golden-oldie station warbling out of my alarm-clock radio. I marginally knew the late-night disc jockey, a curly haired guy named Johnny, and deemed it no small coincidence we both "worked" the same hours. Johnny was riding the crest of the station's newly won popularity, appearing regularly at supermarket openings, used-car promotions, sorority carnivals. It was mean fame, but fame nonetheless, and I attached to him the mindless identification of the unknown to the known, as if his success were a foretoken of mine, a means of peering into a dark and fog-enshrouded future. One night during a particularly exasperating bout with the story, my brain's word-creating mechanism grinding to a not unfamiliar halt, Johnny's station coincided with a similar blankness, and as I looked at the plastic radio, as though seeking from it explanation, Johnny's voice returned to the air, saying, "That was our silent typewriter there, folks." I turned off the radio, then the lights, returning in the dark to the beanbag and assuming my kneeling position. The Underwood sat before me, a block of shadow. Power was in that machine, power as vast and sweeping and threatening as the night itself, power in the faded keys, the cement blocks, the hardwood floor, in the bare branches scraping the window, the icicles on midnight eaves, the encrusted sidewalk, the moonlit snow, the alleys and rooftops and wind, in the secret night of surrounding man, the night of a silent typewriter.

Two weeks after Robert left I received a letter from Marcia. After a three-year exile she was returning to Minneapolis for a visit, a three-day weekend, one day for each year missed. Would I pick her up at the airport? She'd be staying with

Harry and Linda but they wouldn't be home till late that night and she'd really appreciate it and she admitted she was stoned and a little drunk from a bottle of peach-flavored brandy and this dee-vor-say role was a little hard to get used to...But would I pick her up? And would I get Minneapolis ready to party? Hurry up, divorced lady. Party down, divorced lady. Don't let it be too late.

# 4.

Marcia's letter served as prelude to several events in my life. I had gone out one night and hit the bars on the north side, walking from Irv's to the 200 to Standup Frank's over and over, a wide, looping, irregular orbit. It was a full-moon night, unseasonably warm, and I felt possessed of a gregarious vitality, a sudden outbreak of cabin fever. People were pressed to the bars like piglets to a sow, and I loved it. I wanted to oink and squeal and suck beer, to press against the bar and feel the mobfooted motion circle round it, to slap people on the back and buy them beers and let them buy me beers, to drink greedily of this short-lived full-moon night.

At some point I met Miss Universe. I was drunk, a state, if not adding to my glibness, then at least not deflating my confidence in it. I had watched her play pool, our eyes meeting occasionally. She was tall, wearing black stretch pants and a turquoise bowling shirt. But her hair was what got me, a long flip with parted bangs, reminding me of the mid-Sixties, of plastic go-go boots and mini skirts, of Miss Universe contenders. She would tell me neither her name nor where she was from. But she did return with me to my room.

But I could do nothing that night. Later, as we lay in bed and smoked cigarettes, I mentally tallied the reasons for such a flagging — the consumption of beer and other substances, the lateness of the hour, the impersonality of Miss Universe.

The impotence itself didn't bother me. I had learned my lesson about drinking and sex long ago, having while in the army paid a hooker twenty dollars for the privilege of throwing up in her toilet. But a strangeness suffused this particular interlude, a threat of potential symbolism, as if I'd lately been courting some beguiling celestial force, had been buoyed by the promise of consummation—in whatever form it might take—and had been somehow cheated.

Alice invited me to supper one night, asking beforehand if I would talk to Ralph. They just weren't making it, she explained. Ralph had yet to sell one set of encyclopedias, and here the baby was due in a matter of weeks, and what were they going to for money? Ralph had to get a job, a real job, but he was just too darn stubborn.

The forthcoming burdens and responsibilities were apparently not lost on Ralph. All through supper he had been quiet, feeding himself with one hand while leaning his head on the other, staring at his plate as though it were the void. After supper I asked him how business was going. He said he had almost made a sale a few days ago, but at the last minute the lady balked. "It was my own fault," he concluded. "I didn't apply the techniques correctly." I disagreed. I said anyone would find it damn hard to sell those things, especially now when times were so tight. People couldn't afford such luxuries. Ralph, staring down this whole time, now looked up at me, an expression of rehearsed disbelief on his face: "You're saying education is a *luxury*?"

I later told Alice not to worry (who was I, the Ann Landers of Northeast?), that it looked like Ralph was finally starting to see things for himself. Things always work out, I told her. Always.

Even my story was working out. I had excreted three drafts and now felt nothing but blank numbness. I found that upon writing a piece over and over, harrying sentence after sentence, examining all with Cyclopean perspective, I eventually could not read what was before me, my mind seeing words a split-second before my eyes. Consequently, I had no idea if the story was good or bad. I remember thinking that after three drafts it had to be good. One paragraph, at least, describing the passage of a motorcycle gang, seemed to rise above the level of mediocrity:

> They went on run that weekend, and once again Ranger felt the pride, the tingling freedom, of running with the pack. Ranger and Frank were in front, riding the crest of a huge, thundering and unstoppable wave, a wave that ate pavement with a massive speed and unappeased hunger, and cared not for the right or left or behind but only forward, forward, forward, and Ranger's heart, after five long years, beat once again with the rhythm of the pack, and he felt he had come home.

Though even then acknowledging a Wolfean influence on my prose, years would pass before I realized not only syntax and structure but plot itself was lifted from the giant North Carolinian's work; "Good Days Past" — about a biker returning to his old gang after five years in jail, only to find he could no longer abide with the old-new ways — was but a motorcycle version of *You Can't Go Home Again*! But all similarities to Wolfe ended there. His characters fairly turned the pages of the book for you. Mine wouldn't give you the time of day. My characters had all the life of cardboard. My characters just didn't give a shit.

After performing what were amounting to rituals, painstakingly labeling the envelopes, sheathing and resheathing the manuscript, licking the dry glue with grim finality, I walked to the mailbox on Central Avenue. I did not know if the story swallowed by that blue maw was good or bad or somewhere in between.

That night, while lying in bed, hands interlaced behind my neck, I pondered what I had done. What did it mean to work on a story day after day, to drag it through untold layers of resistance, to stare and mull and struggle, then sheath it in manila and shoot it along the postal orbits to the desk of a stranger, to have this stranger hold, page through, presumably read, and ultimately pass judgement on those sheets of sweat? Why had I entered so unthinkingly on such a path?

# 5.

A few days later I found a letter from Robert in my mail slot. Receiving returned manuscripts (always with the slight shock of recognizing my own handwriting), the delicious protraction of examining the sealed envelope, had fostered a habit of examining all mail before opening, myself adopting a kind of Holmesian posture, as if I could glance at a gas bill and pop up with, "Ah, I see the postman is left-handed." I studied Robert's letter. The return address was Unit 4F, Ward Seven, Johns Hopkins Hospital, Baltimore, Maryland. I immediately "deduced" that Robert had either fallen ill or gotten in an accident. The deduction evolved into fantasy. Laid up in the hospital, a limb or two in traction, Robert was visited daily by Marcia. She quickly fell in love with him, and he was writing now to invite me to their wedding.

Of course all this was wrong. Opening the envelope and deciphering what passed as Robert's handwriting, a mishmash of printed and written words, arrows and strike-outs and cartoon figures, I found that Robert had yet to even see Marcia, much less declare his love, and that he was in the hospital not as a patient but as a research subject. Having arrived in Baltimore void of money, Robert engaged upon one of the strangest and most challenging episodes of his life.

Staying with Freddie, of all people (who knew nothing of Robert's infatuation with his ex-wife), Robert spotted an ad in the Baltimore Sun for research subjects. The pay was thirty dollars a day, plus room and board. Attending a screening process, Robert and other prospects were told the experiment involved ingesting diarrhea serum. Stomach cramps, dizziness, uncontrollable and simultaneous vomiting and defecating was in store. They could not leave once the project began, and no one volunteered twice.

Freddy, psychopharmacologist that he was, had heard the horror stories and tried to deter Robert from his plans. They went out to eat crabs the night before the experiment, Freddie listing reason after nauseating reason why Robert should find some other way to make money. Finally, Robert held up his hand and said, "Yas, yas, yas, I spose everbody'll be real sick alright, but I...ain't going to get it." Freddie at first laughed, then "studied" Robert to see if he was serious. He was. "It's all very simple," Robert explained. "I'll simply zen the diarrhea away."

Here Robert confessed (in the letter) to not knowing how to zen anything. But he wrote at length about "mind control" and "mind over matter" and an "exercise of will." He reminded me of how he had willed away hay fever one spring, despite a doctor's assertion he would have the catarrh once a year the rest of his life. This would be a more definitive test. If, under the unblinking gaze of empirical science, Robert remained standing while all those around fell, credence would have to be granted to his beliefs or, as he put it, the ol' Robert Method of Mind Control.

The method, Robert wrote, was outwardly simple. Upon rising and retiring, and once at midday, he would clear his mind of all thoughts, all internal dialogue (had he learned this in India?), and concentrate on a single unworded concept, in this case the prevention of diarrhea.

So on February 10, 1980 Robert and fourteen others were locked in the seventh ward of Johns Hopkins Hospital and, in a scene evocative of the Guyana Jonestown massacre, one by one drank Dixie cups of diarrhea serum. Within three days, they were told, the symptoms would manifest. "Eat, drink and be merry," wrote Robert, "for tomorrow we puke." His letter ended on the third day of the test, and already people were moaning and holding their stomachs. Robert so far felt great but acknowledged that only "time would tell."

Did such beliefs belong in the twentieth century? Not that I was qualified to judge. The submission of my latest story revived all the dormant superstitions, the plethora of omens both sought and created. Logic and rationality were poor substitutes for entrails casting. And what about Robert's "method?" What were words? Did they come from thought or create it? Or somehow both? A child discovers words. Words discover the child. To children words are magic, rhyming arrows, arcane missiles. Don't say it. It might happen.

Two weeks later I was sitting in a borrowed Buick on Post Road, watching planes descend from purple twilight. In half an hour Marcia would arrive. I had written Robert about her visit, though I had received no reply. According to his timetable, he would be released from the hospital today. What would his course of action be? Was Robert even now hurtling across the continent?

# 6.

I awoke the next morning with a headache. Marcia lay beside me, her breathing deep and regular, lips slightly parted. I lit a cigarette. I had not lain with a woman in the morning for a long time.

Marcia had looked damn good walking down the terminal at the airport, waving to me, her long hair and tweed coat flaring behind. We went downtown (Marcia playing a hick and walking neck-craned and gawking at the gleaming, spiring buildings) and up to the observation deck of the IDS tower, there to oversee the cardinal points, the Mississippi river fish-grey and twisting, St. Paul a glowing hulk to the east, a trace of sunset dying in the west. I slipped my arm round Marcia's waist.

I now lay very still, occasionally bringing the cigarette to my mouth, then tapping it against the ashtray on my stomach — a smoker's universe, the red pack of Pall Malls, the metal lighter, the glass ashtray. Morning light shot through cracks in the window shade, spotlighting dustmotes in lazy circumlocution. It all reminded me of my ill-fated, short-lived encounter (I could scarce call it "affair") with Jody Hollister. Jody had lived in an attic apartment in east St. Paul, a tiny place with angled ceilings and floral wallpaper, a wooden dresser and four-poster bed. I always woke before Jody and liked to lie smoking cigarettes while watching the room fill with light. For reasons now only vaguely remembered, I found pleasure in pretending we were Winston Smith and Julia from Orwell's *1984*. Jody's place reminded me of the flat Smith had rented from Mr. Charrington, a pocket of sanity, of old-fashioned contentment. Somewhere, beyond the recessed windows and lace curtains, were the thought police, waiting to take us to the looming and pyramidic Ministry of Truth. Our time together was precious. Like Smith, I clung instinctively to this resting place of, if not love, then at least communion.

But the fantasy always dissipated upon rising. We were much too free, too burdened by a lack of restraints, to sustain any idea of thought police. Jody working only occasionally and myself not at all, we passed the days—this was Indian summer, the leaves at their height of coloration—riding around in Jody's oil-guzzling Dodge Dart, visiting friends, borrowing money, getting high. Those warm short days held no place for the cold and comforting martyrdom of *1984*.

Our relationship lasted no longer than the autumn leaves. Jody's boyfriend, a hulking fellow Jody had "forgotten" to tell me about, returned one night from some mysterious trip south of the border. Finding myself literally on the streets, I slept a few cold nights in my car, rain and wind decimating the autumn foliage, and eventually moved in under the largess of my friends near campus.

Now, lying next to Marcia, the Winston Smith fantasy returned. Like Smith I had betrayed a friend, had sacrificed my integrity, though Smith had more persuasive reasons than I. No rat-cage mask had been placed on my face; I had not been starved and bludgeoned and kicked until consenting to go to bed with Marcia. It had been an act of free will—by some definitions the worst sin of all.

When I was seven or eight years old I attended my first funeral, that of a relative on my mother's side, a man in his late forties who had died in a boating accident. Having walked with my father to the front of the church and viewed the body, I was surprised at not feeling the emotions I had expected — sorrow, revulsion, fear — just a merely sated curiosity as to what a real (not televised) dead person looked like. I was, however, awed by the solemnity of the occasion, the hushed murmuring, the array of dark clothing, the occasional and out-of-place grin, and I fully expected something magical to happen, as if this is how adults take care of death, my boy. The murmuring quieted, and the dead man's mother entered from the back of the church.

She was old and enormously fat, escorted by a younger woman. Oblivious to the stares of sympathy, of disgust, of whatever, the matriarch made her way down the aisle, taking each step with trepidation, a plump hand grasping the top of each pew, till reaching the end of the pews and entering a kind of free fall, coming to rest before the casket. She stared for a few seconds at her son, then was escorted to a bank of folding chairs off to the side of the altar, there to sit flanked by family members for the remainder of the service.

I watched her for a long time, her plump and pasty countenance cast not in sorrow but in apathy, as if she had all the appreciation of a dog for the events around her. This did not jibe with my idea of motherhood, and I felt an unfamiliar fear. I would see that look again in life, in derelicts on city streets, patients in psychiatric wards, farm people living too long alone, their lives unreeled between sky and earth, the wind blowing in from the west and laying touch upon an inner coldness, a coldness that is a siege.

What scared me most about the mother of the dead man was that, though having never seen that look before, I nonetheless recognized it, felt it stirred within my own being. I became aware that day of a part of myself I did not like, had not wanted to acknowledge, as I did this morning with my cigarettes and sunlight. I would face life with evermore vulnerability, would shield this vulnerability with rising cynicism. Orwell's book had shattered my Pollyanna view of fiction, of life for that matter, not adding so much as subtracting. I had lost something that day of the funeral, as I had this morning lying next to Marcia, lying in bed and smoking cigarettes, waiting for the thought police.

# 7.

I never heard from Robert again. Plugging three dollars of change into the pay phone at Momart's one night, I called Freddie in Baltimore. Robert had indeed stayed the onslaught of diarrhea. "Oh, you mean the zen master," Freddie said. Among the volunteers, Robert alone had not contracted the disease, spending those seventeen days, aside from the foul odors and Dantesque moans of the less psychically developed, in comfort, reading, watching television, eating as much as he wanted. I asked how Marcia was. She was fine, still working, still taking care of their kid. Robert had left for parts unknown, refusing to tell where he was bound.

The morning after our tension-filled coupling (at least tension-filled for me; I had half-expected Robert to come banging on my door the whole time), lying in bed and staring at the ceiling, I told Marcia of Robert's love, of how he must never know what happened, of how I had betrayed my best friend. Marcia listened to all this quietly, seeming neither sympathetic nor particularly interested. I didn't press it. The whole thing was one big hollow drama, like a ride on a Ferris wheel.

I did not see her after that, Marcia returning to Baltimore two days later. I learned through Freddie that Robert had received my letter, and I had to assume he waited for Marcia, though what happened then I can only speculate. I choose to think Robert presented Marcia with his love, had been turned down, the hook of love pushed all the way through, but at least he knows, my wan and feeble advice, and now roams the highways, his sorrow and fury and passion unreeling behind, soaking into the earth, repositor of all feeling, all sadness, all life.

And life broke anew in the apartment above me. It was a day of high comedy, Ralph assuming every worry and ludicrous posture of every husband in every sitcom and comic-strip and celluloid waiting room. I was walking up to the rooming house one afternoon when Ralph yelled at me from his window. I was to come quick! Alice was having the baby right now! Ralph met me halfway on the stairs, dragging me by the arm into his apartment. I had visions of afterbirth and placenta, of some red slimy miniature human writhing on Mrs. McAdams' carpet. Inside was utter, tangible, and unexpected silence, and in the midst of that silence, reclining on a davenport like Mae West, cow-like contentment on her features, was Alice. Let Ralph do all the worrying. That's what he's good at. Labor had set in that morning, she told me, and they would call a taxi in a while. No hurry. Sit down. Ralph ran into the kitchen, returning with a flaccid wedge of lemon meringue pie, devouring it in three bites. Ralph explained he'd been eating all day long he was so nervous, ever since the contractions had started, and I'd better believe there was such a thing as sympathy pains...

Ralph suddenly turned pale. He ran into the bathroom and audibly threw up, great, retching, vaudevillian groans, an empathic and pseudo-birth. Alice and I laughed uncontrollably, Ralph yelling at us to shut up. Eventually they left in a yellow cab for St. Mary's Hospital. A birth in the spring, a good omen.

Other omens were not quite so encouraging. The biker story seemed to have been out considerably longer than the others—again, I had failed to note the date of submission—and I grew increasingly anxious as to its fate. As winter faded and spring bloomed, I found myself thinking of the story constantly, of that one shining paragraph. Reasoning, with logic I cannot remember, that the longer the piece was out the better its chances of acceptance, I took each daily no-show, each unanswered trip to the foyer, as evidence the odds were increasing in my favor. I read and reread stories in back issues of *Easyriders, Iron Horse, Cycle,* inevitably finding mine vastly superior. But such self-aggrandizement was at its core hollow, a glass obelisk that, far from being strengthened by the protracted mystery, grew evermore shard-like, evermore brittle.

A pattern emerged. Once again sessions at the typewriter were sporadic, short-lived. My attention possessed all the staying power of a butterfly, tapping out first lines, possible titles, idiotic plot ideas. How could one lousy story be so important?

More than ever, I questioned my qualifications. What was I lacking? Had I not at least average intelligence? Why did I kick blameless furniture, crumple sheets of innocent paper, inhale cigarettes with suicidal rapture? Was this being a writer?

Reasoning that the whole situation, my monumental contraction of writer's block, this time a "block" inundating every facet of my life, personified ultimately by my inability to put words to paper, stemmed entirely from the unknown fate of my latest submission, I decided to put an active hand in matters. I would write a letter. Though this violated an inner code of stoicism—never let editors know you care—I deemed it a move necessary for artistic survival. Unexpectedly, enthusiasm returned, and I set out to write a letter with a casual, flippant tone, economically chatty, and oh by the way, did my latest story happen to cross your desk?

Just a little something I whipped up the other day. Completely academic interest, you understand.

I spent an entire day writing the letter of inquiry, going through five or six drafts before deigning it worthy of my signature. Everpresent was the fear the story may have been tottering between acceptance and rejection, and that my letter could shift the balance either way. Dropping it in the mailbox, I felt, rather than the sinking dread accompanying my submissions, an unexpected relief. The act felt clean, and my outlook became increasingly optimistic.

Two days later I found my manuscript jutting from the mail slot.

# 8.

April heralded the lushest, most verdant spring I could remember. Everywhere was solar promise, lengthening days and blue-chalk skies, clouds fresh-scrubbed and hung out to dry. Cars were washed in driveways, gardens planted, shorts donned — this noted on my infrequent walks. I stayed inside a lot, spending entire mornings and afternoons on my bed, my thoughts like feeble blips from a distant planet.

Rejection. All the omens, all the mind games, jabbing the lightstring three times, the overheard conversations, peering into the foyer, all my shields in effect, had been stripped away. Despite having convinced myself the outcome would not matter, that failing in this latest attempt would lessen not a whit my determination, I now experienced a vapid and vast loss of energy, as if a plug had been removed and all my power, all my resolve, had irretrievably drained away. The unexpectedness of this demoralization had caught me defenseless, and I could construct no rationalization convincing enough to allow me comfort.

Enter depression. Enter lost meaning of life. Enter seasonal reminder of days more innocent and promising, an anniversary by which to mark not only time but defeat.

Three years earlier I said goodbye to my mother and father and brother at the Little Rock bus depot. Having helped my brother move to my parents', riding with him in his rust-eaten

Chevy from Minnesota to Arkansas while engaging in theological debates, I now realized I was returning alone to our ancestral homeland. Through the window I could see my family, standing with the shuffling stillness of people in home movies, their faces solemn. I forced myself to smile. They smiled back, and for that moment everything was somehow *right*. Then the bus lurched forward and pulled out of the cement cavern and my family was gone.

I hunched down in the seat, leaning against the window. Across the aisle sat a young black woman. She was pretty, slender, intelligent-looking, and I was to spend mile after unreeling mile trying to force myself to speak to her. Fearful of southern taboos (though in truth we could have been on the moon and I would have come up with some reason not to approach her), I wound up doing nothing. I had enough to think about anyway, this being the delicious start of a trip, the sadness of farewell dissipating and the adventure of the road ahead.

We lumbered north, stopping every few miles at towns of varying size and description. This was irritating, slowing down and pulling over just when the bus seemed to be underway, and I grew slightly nauseous under the diesel thrum of boredom, my body yearning for motion. The driver, a red-haired stocky man, seemed as frustrated by these stops as I, his expression and demeanor that of haste, loading baggage into the side compartments, fairly leaping back aboard, winding the bulbously streamlined bus to seventy miles an hour on the straightaways, constantly glancing at the road and mirrors, fearful of his watch. Eventually, as the sun sank and towns and houses fell behind, darkness settling, we were finally really underway, the driven driver still pushing it at seventy. I huddled up and stared out the window into blackness.

Night! Like Wolfe's George Webber I had always "loved the night more dearly than the day." In the night all are equal.

In the night one can cry, and hide, do shameful deeds, and there is solitude, respite from prying eyes, eyes that had been on me before birth, the anonymity of a city is in the night, and the sidewalks stretch down lonely streets with television windows, and the dogs chained out back are us, and I say goodbye to my family in the rushing night, the same night we traversed on our family vacations, so frail and innocent in the brown Pontiac, and I'd just as soon ride every trip of my life at night, an eternal black highway I could return to, always.

At three in the morning I had to transfer, spending an hour in the St. Louis bus depot, sitting in an orange fiberglass chair, sipping rancid coffee while watching a milling parade of farm folk, poor folk, servicemen, janitors, schizophrenics, drunks, college kids, pseudo pimps, and other travelers of the American night. The place had a bleakness about it, an echoing gymnasium sterility that suffused both atmosphere and people, manifest in the bitter coffee, the cigaretted floor, the ocean-like murmur, in the school-house clocks that were on every wall, minute hands sweeping silently, as if time actually meant something, and the clocks spoke for everyone, saying let's get this trip and shift and night over with and just go home, wherever that may be.

Morning found us in northern Missouri, the bus once again snagging at hole-in-the-wall depots, white-washed crackerboxes with faded Dr. Pepper signs. The day quickly became warm and muggy, and I grew all too conscious of my unwashed condition, the grittiness of too little sleep, eyes scratchy, mouth fuzzy. The driver announced we would stop for breakfast in half an hour. I steeled myself for the wait. An internal rebellion was fomenting in my limbs, my body balking at inactivity. For distraction I began to take note of my fellow passengers.

A young Amish couple sat near the front, a baby girl balanced on the woman's knee. They must have boarded sometime after St. Louis, during one of my periods of "sleep", though I would have sworn to have not slept at all that night. The man, despite his beard, or maybe because of it, seemed inordinately young; both he and the woman I assumed was his wife seemed too young, an air of optimism about them that was almost sickening, their scrub-faced naivete, the promise of hope on the woman's bouncing knee, their edge-of-seat eagerness, their bus ride to death, the white-line divide other side.

We stopped for breakfast. Afterwards, walking back to the bus from the cafe, my path crossed with the Amish man's. He asked if I'd had a good breakfast. His inquiry had been so earnest and the morning light so warm and generous, the powder-blue sky and muggy air and drooping vegetation suddenly possessed of a wondrous vitality, the oppressiveness of the St. Louis night finally sloughing off, that I could do not but return his smile and answer that, yes, I had had a good breakfast.

We spent the rest of the morning winding more or less northwards as I marked progress on my Rand McNally road atlas, passing through Eolia, Flinthill, Keokuk, and the uninhabited places between those dots on the map, the foliage green and sultry, married to summer like a new bride, glimpses of dirt paths with overhanging trees, faded Coke signs on lonely posts, the sudden bright treelessness of plowed fields, reaching the river towns of southern Iowa, Montrose, Fort Madison, the bus becoming more crowded with each stop till finally in Burlington I am joined by a young man on his way to Minneapolis where he and his friend — that's Buck right in front of us — (Buck turns and smiles) will compete in the Midwest Foosball Tournament. The two are eighteen, maybe nineteen, wearing jeans and plaid shirts with rolled-up sleeves, a pair of black-framed glasses perpetually sliding down my companion's nose. I find myself listening with interest as he talks about his and Buck's chances in the upcoming tournament, how much they've practiced, how they were virtually unbeatable in the bars of Burlington; and I think here's another shot for the common guy, a shortcut chance for fame, for acknowledgement, like winning the last game of pool, hitting a homerun in a pickup softball game, turning a hundred-thousand points on pinball, of hearing someone say, "We know you're there."

But such chances were so miserly, so reeking of spare change, so obviously machinated to make profit for those behind the scenes, that I could feel naught but pity for the participants. In a world reshaped daily by headlines, that dispersed late at night when the off switch was flipped, what chance had anyone, much less Buck and his friend? How many avenues lay open to the towering obelisk of fame?

Around noon the bus lumbered into the Muscatine depot and I disembarked. The sole clerk at the depot let me use the phone, then shooed me out, explaining he had to lock up and go to lunch. I sat on my suitcase in the dirt parking lot, watching ants until my friend, John, showed up. He dropped me off at his and his wife's house, then returned to his job. This was the Friday of a Memorial Day weekend, and the plan was for John, myself, and several others to caravan from the cornfields of southern Iowa to the forests of northern Minnesota. After showering at John's, I walked into the livingroom, intending to pass the time before my next departure by drinking beer and leafing through old copies of *Playboys*. I happened to notice a notepad near the telephone, and I can't remember if I thought of it right then or if the idea had been bubbling in the back of my head for years, but I picked up the notepad and started writing about the trip I was on. I kept writing the entire weekend, every chance I got, eventually filling up the notepad and continuing my saga on a school-type notebook purchased in a drugstore in Duluth.

Two months later, I had a short novel on my hands. I was hooked.

But this original wellspring of creation, this torrent of giddy industriousness, had by now slowed to a pathetic trickle. Attempts at writing became exercises in despair, and I would search ceaselessly for something else to do: taking a walk, playing guitar, drinking, reading (though here the guilt crept back), anything to hasten the sunset and an excuse to go to bed. The Underwood sat on its cement podium, like some fondly remembered brain-dead relative. I hadn't the heart to stow the typewriter in the back of some closet, to pull the plug, as it were, but also I could not bring myself to disturb the dust slowly accreting upon its forty-nine keys.

I reread the biker story only a few times, each time enveloped by an embarrassment bordering upon shame. If I could not get published in a biker magazine—a goddamn biker magazine—then what chance had I for the other markets, much less my even loftier goal of literary recognition? After twelve months of "serious" writing, of shooting for the acid test of publication, I now found myself standing before a chasm of personal failure.

And then, upon returning home one depressingly bright and sunny day, I noticed a manila-sized envelope sticking out from my mail slot. The return address was from *Iron Horse*. For a moment the world stopped. I knew I had sent them only one story. Hadn't I? My mind raced to an improbable fantasy—perhaps the editors had had a change of heart! "You rejected 'Good Days Past?'" I imagined one of them bellowing at an underling. "Get in contact with this Matthews fellow immediately, if he'll even have us, that is!"

Of course I didn't open the envelope for hours, relishing, as in the days before, the sweet drip of mystery. And of course during those hours I could think of nothing else until, finally, standing in the rays of sunset slanting through my western window, I slowly tore open the flap and discovered the contents to be another folded envelope and a single sheet of paper.

It was not a form letter. My name did not appear in dark type behind "dear." It was an actual letter written by a flesh-and-blood editor. My knees grew weak. So such creatures did exist! This is what the letter said:

Dear Mr. Matthews:
Rumor has it that mail is carried over the Rockies by a small dog with a large cart, and he eats anything he doesn't want to carry. I do hope you retained a copy of your magnificent story, as it never, to the best of my knowledge, ever arrived here. All manuscripts are routed to me and neither your name nor the title of the story sound familiar. I am enclosing an envelope addressed to me. If possible, would you send another manuscript? This over-the-transom system yields so much terrible fiction that I would be delighted to read a magnificent story anytime!
I do hope that you won't succumb to a life of crime—but if it should come to that, some of best, most reliable writers are in prison.
Write to live,
L.- - - - - - -
Associate Editor

Hope returned instantly and my head reeled. An editor had actually contacted me! But what to do? I certainly couldn't resubmit the original story, not that piece of garbage. But neither could I ignore the letter, this gauntlet tossed. I glanced at the Underwood, a block of shadow in the gathering dusk. I knew I would not return to it that night, nor the next, but someday, a day of rain perhaps, with coffee on the stove and cigarettes in the pack, a sheet of paper virgin-white and the whole world ahead.

Printed in the United States
69109LVS00002B/12